Ripped, Stripped and Flipped

She hit the numbers on the phone precisely, leaving no room for error. She had memorized the number for Roberts' private line when he had given it to her earlier.

"Detective Roberts."

She heard the gruff voice through the background noise at the Police Bureau.

"I've got another one."

"One what?" asked Detective Roberts. "Illegal parker, graffiti artist?"

"No. No. Of course not. A ..."

"Ms. Howard, you're going to have to work with me here. Two syllables? Starts with?" he asked, trying to help her.

"A body."

"Of course you do. That's why you had to beat off Swensen at the bar," he said calmly.

Obviously, the story had spread.

"No. A dead body!"

"Are you sure?" he asked.

"There's blood and it didn't move when I screamed at it."

"Is it someone you know?"

"I don't think so."

"And, it sounds like it may be too late for introductions," he said. "Again."

Ripped, Stripped and Flipped

KATHLEEN HERING

Published November 2013
By Kathleen Hering
Albany, Oregon

.

ISBN-10: 149294405X
ISBN: 13 978-1492944058

For
hh

1

"911. What is your emergency?"

"Oh good, you're home."

"We're always home, Ma'am.   What is your emergency?"

"I want to give you a hand."

"And the Portland Police Bureau appreciates that. We really do. Now what is your emergency?"

"I found a hand."

"Can you be more specific, Ma'am?"

"I came outside to check on some concrete we poured late yesterday and I found this hand."

"This is 911 Emergency Services. We don't routinely consider a handprint in new concrete as an emergency."

"Not a print," she said. "A human hand. It's sticking out of the fresh pour from yesterday."

"What is your address?"

"I'm on the Street of Dreams."

"Of course you are." The dispatcher paused briefly. "Is there by any chance a street number where you are?"

She gave him the number she saw painted in red on a piece of plywood balanced against the curb at the construction site.

"I have a car on the way, Ma'am. Please stay on the line. Let me know when you hear the sirens approaching."

Laura continued to pace in the street along the curb. The Graham Construction partners had been flattered when they'd been asked to remodel the original house on the property where this year's Street of Dreams show houses were to be constructed. Now she wasn't so thrilled.

"Are you still there, Ma'am?"

Laura nodded—which didn't tell the dispatcher a thing.

"Have I lost you?" he asked.

"Still here."

"While you're waiting, could you describe the hand to me?"

"It's covered with cement."

"Left or right hand?"

"I can't tell."

"Check the thumb." This caller was in shock, nuts or drunk. Sometimes they got all three in the same call, he thought. "The right hand is the one with the thumb on the left."

That only works on living people looking at their own hands from above, but the dispatcher didn't care. It just came out.

"Left, then. And he's single." She'd spent most of her twenties sneaking a peek to see if a man had an indentation on a finger where an absent wedding band usually rested but had been removed for an instant guy's night out.

"You think it's a man's hand? Caucasian or person of color?" he asked.

"White, but not a warm white, a soft icy white with a gray tinge," she said. "It would be better for a bathroom than the main rooms in a house."

"Say what?"

"I hear sirens."

"Thank God."

"A little prayer can help when choosing paint for an accent wall. There's a difference between being brave and going crazy." Laura Howard, Decorator

2

Laura Howard was shaken. She was too upset to stay at the work site to continue working on her decorating sketches, but not so overwhelmed that she couldn't drive to Graham Construction to let her business partners know about her discovery at the Dreams site.

She would have phoned them, but she knew Russ was taking the morning off to watch the news of the hurricane approaching the East Coast. Esther had plans to give a bath to Hammer, the large sheepdog who was their unofficial fourth partner.

Laura knocked on the side door at Graham Construction.

Russ opened the door, and looked at her quizzically.

"Since when do you knock before you walk in?" he asked.

"I don't know," she said. "I guess I just appreciate having hands this morning." She smiled weakly. Then she held up both of her hands and waved at him.

"It's before noon. Have you been drinking?" Russ asked.

"No, but we may want to put on a pot of coffee. The police will be here in about an hour to tell us more about the hand I found—the one they think could be attached to a body. They're digging at our construction site right now."

Russ led Laura to a chair. He watched her carefully. She seemed sober, but how could you really tell?

Esther Graham strolled into the office, and Russ signaled to her not to say anything. He didn't want Laura sidetracked before he heard the rest of what she had to report. Interior decorator Laura, builder Russell Graham, and his outspoken aunt and bookkeeper Esther had been through a lot together since forming their home construction and remodeling company. Russ knew Esther would want to hear whatever this was first hand.

"Don't say hand!" he reprimanded himself silently.

"Let me summarize for you, Esther," he said. "Laura says the police are due here any minute to tell us more about a possible body . . ." He stopped. "It was dead, wasn't it, Laura?"

"Dead and buried."

". . . about a body Laura may have found this morning at the construction site."

"I knew we shouldn't have accepted that job," Esther said.

"Kind of a moot point now," he said. "We're in deep."

"So was the body," Laura added quietly.

Russ shook his head. He loved Laura, but was the woman turning into a murder magnet? It wasn't long ago that she had helped the police unravel the details around her husband Todd's death and the deaths of some of his associates.

The doorbell rang and Laura jumped. Russ went to open the door.

A uniformed officer and another man, a detective apparently, came in. Russ suggested they gather around the dining room table and Esther poured coffee in ceramic mugs without bothering to take individual orders from anyone.

The man in plain clothes was 38 or 40. He was wearing a blue blazer, gray Dockers, and a yellow tie against a white shirt.

"I'm Detective Leonard Roberts," he said. He turned to Russ. "Can you tell me about that construction project of yours on the Street of Dreams?" he asked.

"Every year," Russ said, "contractors build homes on a block-long street selected by our greater Portland area home builders' association. It's an honor to be asked to participate in an Oregon Street of Dreams project, and it's a way for us to see what new products and building techniques are out there and to show off our own skills. After open house in August, the homes are listed with local real estate offices and sold."

He looked at the detective. Is that what the man wanted to know, Russ wondered.

"The house where I met Ms. Howard this morning didn't look like new construction," the uniformed officer put in. "By the way, I'm William Anderson," he added.

"It's not," Russ said. "This year the association decided to leave the original house on the property and let one of us tackle remodeling it. Graham Construction got that honor."

The detective spoke up. "You do know you may have to stop work for a few days, don't you?" he asked.

"Laura told us that there's trouble out there," Russ said. "Maybe you could be more specific."

"Ms. Howard says she went out to check on a concrete slab you poured late yesterday. Can you confirm that?" the detective asked.

Laura, Russ and Esther nodded.

"At 9:17 a.m. today we got an Emergency Services 911 call from one Laura Howard reporting she had found a suspicious object buried in concrete," he continued.

"It wasn't an 'object,'" Laura said. "It was a hand."

"Right."

"Left," Laura corrected.

Russ sighed deeply.

"As Ms. Howard was leaving, a city crew arrived and dug up the body," the detective continued. The cops had suspected that they were at a crime scene, he explained, but had gotten Laura out of there before the body was brought to the surface.

"There was more than the hand, then?" Laura asked.

"Plenty more. The deceased was completely—er, together—nicely clothed, black dress shoes, and had all of his ID, money and credit cards on him. It made identification a snap."

Laura looked at her coffee mug. She thought she was going to be sick, but was afraid the cup wouldn't catch it all. She mumbled an excuse and made a dash for the kitchen sink and barfed up the breakfast burrito special she had eaten on the way to the site. She cleaned herself up, and returned to the dining room. (The lyrics from "Bounty, the quicker picker upper" circled in her brain, but she hoped that was her brain in protection mode rather than disrespect for the dead.) She strained to pay attention to the turn the conversation had taken.

"Do any of you know a Sal Martinelli?" the officer asked.

"The name doesn't sound familiar," Esther said. "Should we know her?"

Laura listened carefully as the officer explained that Sal Martinelli was a man—a very specific man. Salvador Albert Martinelli. The man whose hand Laura had spotted partially buried in the wide sweep of concrete in front of the Dreams house.

"He was familiar to the police," the detective said. "The guy was a small-time local criminal with a list of convictions going clear back to the early 80s. When I talked to the chief this morning, he recalled that Martinelli had been involved in a scam operation, ripping off independent cab drivers," Roberts said. "Apparently there wasn't enough evidence to indict him."

"I've heard the name before, too," Anderson said. "He's always on the outer edge of our radar screen. No mob ties that anyone knows of, but linked to shady players."

"He flies—or flew—just under the radar," Roberts added.

"Looks like he hit an air pocket," Esther suggested quietly.

"I can't say I was surprised that someone put a bullet through him."

"They shot him through the driveway?" Laura asked.

"They shot him through the heart. We think he was dead before they dumped him."

Laura paled.

"Do you know anybody who would rather you weren't working there?" Officer Anderson asked the three of them.

No one nodded.

"Anybody disgruntled that you got the job instead of them?"

No one answered.

"I thought the hand meant he was trying to climb *out* when the concrete hit him," Laura said.

"It was a 9 mm bullet that hit him," the detective said. "That's our best guess until we get the ballistics tests. It's possible that he was killed four to six hours before they delivered him to you folks and covered him over." He cleared his throat. "We think someone may have left his hand out as a warning to you. A very serious warning."

Officer Anderson edged toward the door.

"We've probably got all the information we need for now," the detective said. "You'll need to stay in town. We'll want to question you throughout this investigation. We may be back as early as tomorrow afternoon."

Laura signed her statement for the police, but she had forgotten part of the routine. Without even a slight apology, the officer asked for her full name, age, hair and eye color, height, and *weight* for the blanks at the top of the form.

"Laura Howard, 29, auburn, green, five foot eight," she said.

He waited patiently for the remaining information.

"134," she mumbled.

"IT'S NOT LIKE SOMEONE set fire to my car," Laura said when the investigators returned the next day.

The detective looked puzzled. He had returned to the Graham Construction site to ask additional questions of Laura and the Grahams.

Russ had spent his day brooding about not being allowed on his own construction site and putting together preliminary bids for their next possible job.

Laura had spent hers worrying. She was trying to calm herself when the cops called to say they wanted to meet the three of them out at the Dreams site. She called Russ and Esther and they got to the site as the Portland police car arrived out front.

"Have you given this matter more thought?" the detective asked Laura.

"Yes. Every minute since you pulled away from the curb yesterday," she said.

"And?" he prompted her.

"I don't know what to think," she said. "It's not like last time when somebody broke into my house. And, from what you told us, they only killed him once."

The detective's eyes widened, but he stayed silent.

"Maybe *I* should explain," Esther said. "Laura has been through a horrendous past two years. Her husband was killed."

"I'm sorry for your loss," the officer said to Laura.

"And after they killed him the first time," Esther explained, "he harassed Laura by phone. And then someone tried to kill *her*."

"This is supposed to help?" Detective Roberts asked.

"My turn," Russ said with a tone of authority that silenced the others.

Russ summarized the events of the past two years. Laura's late husband Todd Howard had been reported as a homicide victim. After receiving Todd Howard's death certificate, Laura received something even more disturbing: phone messages in her husband's voice. A later phone threat and extortion attempt ended badly.

"Detective Chris Pfeifer can fill you in on the details," Russ added. "He handled the case."

"Thank you!" Detective Roberts said.

He directed any other questions he had to Russ for the next few minutes, then turned back to Laura.

"I think you should take this seriously, Ms. Howard," he said. "I'm afraid someone is threatening you. Again."

"How else would we take a murder?" Esther asked.

Laura sat silently. The detective had a nice, caring tone, but he obviously didn't understand.

"Let me try once more," she said. "I don't *do* scared. I did once and, frankly, I didn't like it. I'm not wasting another year of my life being afraid."

"Be cautious and stay aware of your surroundings," Anderson said. "Call us if you need us."

Roberts gathered his notepad and pen from the table and started to rise.

"Poor Sal," Esther said.

"You seem very sympathetic and rather attached to the victim," the detective said. "I'm going to ask you again. Did you know Sal Martinelli, Mrs. Graham?"

"No. I never met him. Definitely never shook his hand," she said.

"Esther!" Laura gasped.

"Your level of concern seems unusual," Detective Roberts repeated.

"It's the concrete," Esther said. "It's such a cold, hard way to die."

OFFICER ANDERSON CORNERED Russ before they left. He needed to know the name of the company that had poured the cement for Graham Construction. It was important to the police to determine what time the workers left the site and what temperature it had been when they finished the job.

Anyone who'd seen the site after Martinelli was buried knew that the company's careful job had been destroyed in an attempt to cover the body. What Anderson needed to calculate was how long the cement would have taken to dry and, consequently, what time the body had been buried.

"I learned some interesting things," he later told Detective Roberts. "In hot summer weather the concrete sets up quicker. Like in a couple of hours. It can take twelve to twenty-four hours in cold weather."

"That's unless they add hot water to the mix," Roberts said.

"Yeah, that's right," Anderson said. "If you know all about this, why am I making the calls?"

"There's a lot at stake here in figuring out whether he was killed before or after the pour."

"A single yard of concrete can weigh two tons," Anderson said.

"Is that how much they poured?"

"No." Anderson said. "They poured it extra deep to account for the slope. At a depth of six inches, one yard would cover the 54 square feet. The guy I talked to said they poured and billed for two yards."

"One or two hand-crafted items make a room look warm and friendly. Several make it look like Great Aunt Gert's place."

3

The phone rang.

Laura reached across the bed to the nightstand, picked up the handset and placed it back in its stand. There was no one she wanted to talk to before 7 a.m.

The phone rang again. Once more she picked it up and put it down. A minute later it rang again. She repeated the motion once more.

On the fourth call, she glanced at the caller ID window and saw that it wasn't a telemarketer calling. It was the Portland Police Bureau.

"Hello."

"Don't hang up!" said a gruff voice.

No "hello." No "good morning." No nothing.

"This is Laura Howard."

"Detective Roberts here. Cancel any plans you have for Thursday."

"I don't take orders very well," she said. "Could you start again?"

There was a pause—ten seconds, maybe—before he spoke again.

"Ms. Howard? This is Detective Len Roberts with the Portland Police Bureau," he said. "How are you today?"

"That's better. Much better," she said. "What's up?"

He told her that he wanted her to attend the services for Mr. Martinelli on Thursday afternoon.

"Only if it's closed casket," she said, remembering the concrete beginning to set between the fingers on Mr. Martinelli's hand.

"Ms. Howard . . ."

"Laura," she corrected him.

"Officer Anderson and I will be your escorts. Laura."

"Why do we think this is a good idea?" she asked. "The guy was already dead by the time I met him. "

Roberts explained to Laura that he wanted her to attend the funeral service to see if there was a mourner there whom both Laura and Martinelli might have known.

"We're looking for any kind of connection that would have caused someone to bury Martinelli on your property."

"You're scaring me."

"I'm not trying to do that, but *someone* is definitely trying to scare you," he said. "I told you that the other day. "

"I'm not sure I want to go to the service," Laura said.

"Anderson and I will be there for your protection," he reminded her.

When she didn't respond instantly, he assumed a friendlier tone.

"Could you please clear your calendar for Thursday? We'll be at your place at 2 p.m."

At least he hadn't said 14:00, causing her to quickly try to translate military time.

"DON'T YOU WANT to wear something a little flashier?" Esther asked.

"You and the detective! You both sound like this is a social event. It's a funeral mass."

"Yes, but you never know who might be there."

"I've got a good clue," Laura answered.

"The dead guy?"

"Got it. First try."

"I still think something that shows a little leg. . ."

"Esther, Mr. Martinelli won't care," Laura answered. "And the cops are going there to see if there are any 'people of interest' in the crowd. "

Laura checked herself in the full-length mirror again. Shiny long auburn hair in place. Check. Green eyes flashing. Check. Purse not matching the shoes. Check.

"Perfect for the gawking mourner who never knew the deceased," she thought. She'd humor Esther and wear the pair of out-of-date black patent leather high heels, but she planned to toss them out when she got home. She silently thanked the Fashion Gods for bringing back a lower heel.

"Home" was The Harrington, a 1930s place Laura knew was built from plans in a Sears Roebuck catalog during that decade. It sat up the block from the Graham Construction headquarters.

She had left the obituary announcement on her kitchen table at The Harrington. Now, she picked up the newspaper clipping which gave details about the service for Mr. Martinelli. The funeral mass was scheduled at St. Michael the Archangel church, followed by private interment.

"Is St. Michael's the 1800s red brick church down by the river?" Laura asked. Many of the older buildings in Portland were centered near the Willamette River in the South Waterfront District.

"Yes. That church is older than the city of Portland," Esther said. "Beautiful old building, but it could use some repairs," she added. "You driving?"

"Unfortunately no," Laura said. "I have a police escort."

Detective Roberts phoned to say they'd leave a little earlier than planned to assure they had a parking place at St. Michaels. He was expecting a large crowd because the Portland church was founded originally to serve the town's Italian speaking community.

Esther made a last-minute decision to join the funeral procession and slipped up the block to her apartment to get her black hat.

Ten minutes later Detective Roberts and Will Anderson pulled up in front of the The Harrington in a dark blue, older-model sedan. Esther was disappointed. She had looked forward to a ride in one of the new fleet of Chevy Caprice cars, each painted with a single rose on the door along with the Police Bureau motto "Sworn to Protect. Dedicated to Serve."

Laura was relieved they wouldn't be travelling in a cruiser with the lights flashing and sirens wailing. If she had run out of lifelines on the Millionaire quiz show, she would have felt safe guessing that this car was a Crown Vic.

Roberts wheeled the car smoothly to SW Mill and 5th Street and into the parking lot behind the church.

"Is this the right day?" he asked. The parking lot was empty. He looked around again and checked his watch. "*We're* on time. Let's go in," he said.

They entered the church grounds through the wrought iron gate in the center of the parking lot and, once inside, were directed to the chapel. The officers picked out a pew about two-thirds of the way back. Laura was seated between Roberts and Anderson. Esther had taken a seat up front.

An organist entered quietly and played what Laura assumed was the prelude.

She reached for a hymn book in the rack on the back of the pew in front of her. She skimmed the pages looking for some of the songs she had sung as a child, but the activity didn't take her mind off her assignment here today.

She had agreed to scan the crowd to see if anyone looked familiar to her, but so far only the four of them and the organist had arrived. None looked suspect to her.

The organist was starting the first notes of the prelude for the third time. A side door opened and a man in priestly robes entered and took his place at the side of the altar to wait.

Half an hour after the service was scheduled to begin, the priest rose and greeted those in attendance. All four of them. Then, as though this were not unusual, he began the service which, by Laura's watch, took 41 minutes. He thanked them for coming, and that was it.

No one else had come to see off Sal Martinelli.

"So what was that all about?" Laura asked as they walked back to the car. "Even the person who made funeral arrangements was AWOL."

"He was there," Roberts said.

The two cops looked at each other.

"No one claimed Mr. Martinelli," Anderson said. "Detective Roberts is the one who wrote the obit and arranged for the funeral to see if we could flush out someone."

"How'd that work for you?" Esther asked.

They drove home in silence.

"Silence may be golden, but gold-colored bathroom fixtures left the fashion scene at a fast trot in 1970."

4

"Esther, I need to test your brain," Laura said.

"Good luck on that one."

"I can't get Mr. Martinelli's death off my mind," Laura said. "What if he didn't die like the police think he did? What if he was, say, coming here to tell us something?" Laura asked.

"Like the fact that he had a bullet through his heart?"

"I'm serious. Has anyone else wondered 'why here?'" Laura asked.

"I'm sure the police have," Esther said. "Some crimes never get solved. And, Martinelli's death has been, if you'll excuse me for saying so, a cold case from the start."

TWO DAYS LATER Esther and Laura drove over to the Dreams construction site after the "all clear" call from the Police Bureau. They were eager to see if anything other than the cement parkway had been tampered with when Martinelli was killed.

The yellow crime scene tape had been removed and a quick tour told them there was no apparent damage to the exterior of the house. Laura was relieved for two reasons. There was no added work to do. (Except to re-pour the cement slab.) And, she felt responsible for seeing that the house was restored to the beauty of its earlier days. It had been in the Childers' family since it was built.

Francesca Childers, the most recent owner, had sold the tract of land for the Street of Dreams with the informal understanding that the Italianate home would be bull-dozed. After an inspection by the city building department, though, the developers opted to have the house and grounds restored to give the new neighborhood a sense of historical perspective. Graham Construction had accepted that task.

"Isn't it a little odd to sell property and give orders to the new buyer?" Esther asked. She had never heard of someone selling a house with an agreement that it be demolished.

"It's unusual," Laura said, "but it may have been the only way the woman could bear to part with the property that had been in her family's hands for so long. She and her son Jamen are also building a show home for the Street of Dreams this year," she added.

"Wait," Esther said. "Don't tell me. They're building that stucco monstrosity on the view lot?"

"Well, yes."

"Do they plan to sell to the Duggar clan or the Sister Wives?" Esther was a big fan of reality television.

"Not Mrs. Childers," Laura said. "She's a very refined woman with definite ideas about how that new house should be sited and how much square footage a two-income young couple needs. Luckily, the city wouldn't approve her original plans for a pool on the flat roof," Laura added.

"I suppose she's already chosen names for the 2.3 children the future buyers will have," Esther said. "She may be 'refined,' but she's been too uppity to speak to me when we've passed on the street."

"I think we should give her the benefit of the doubt," Laura said as she parked the truck in front of the Graham Construction project. "She did make these building sites available for the Street of Dreams."

"That's your plan?" Esther asked. "Be nice? That's it?"

"It's not a *plan* exactly. I just think we should take the high road when she acts snippy."

"If I must," Esther conceded.

Laura fumbled in her purse for the key to the house.

"What makes this house 'Italianate' instead of old and cruddy?" Esther asked as they approached the entry.

"The front porch, for one thing," Laura said. She reached to unlock the front door and pointed out the six-inch square post with beveled corners. "Italianate style homes have a relatively simple shape. Usually, they're two story and they look like a crazed cake decorator got hold of the outside," she said. "We're lucky here. The Cake Boss concentrated primarily on the porch areas and window trim."

Esther stepped back two steps and peered up at the house. The white paint was peeling and the porch steps sagged. The former elegance was well-hidden.

"You can identify Italianates by their wide projecting cornices with heavy brackets, plus paired French doors and classic arches inside. Usually they had hipped roofs, bay windows, and stucco over brick chimneys with fancy chimney caps," Laura added.

Esther entered and looked up, inspecting the stairwell to the second story.

"More than you wanted to know?" Laura asked.

"Interesting facts, but not likely to be retained," Esther confessed.

"In America this style was in vogue between 1840 and the early 1890s," Laura continued. "From what I've read, it was a prosperous time in the country and the style signaled to your neighbors that you had both wealth and modern taste."

"It still seems odd they'd build one on the edge of town," Esther said.

"Remember your friend Mrs. Childers?" Laura asked. "Her family could probably afford a townhouse and a country home."

"Sounds greedy to me," said Esther, thinking about how snug she felt in her small apartment over the Graham Construction workshop.

"Queen Anne and Victorian houses soon knocked these out fashion anyway," Laura said.

"So we're putting all this work into a house that's obsolete?"

"Don't say that too loudly," Laura cautioned. "We're trying not to offend Mrs. Childers. She's already ticked that the Bureau of Development and Building Services didn't require us to level the wonderful old place and build something contemporary on the lot."

"DID YOU HEAR, Russ, why the Childers woman wanted this house destroyed?" Laura asked when he entered the room.

"Nope," Russ answered. The three Graham Construction partners were sweeping the sawdust from the wood flooring in the downstairs of the house before leaving for the weekend and some needed rest.

"Maybe she got stood up at the altar after some fool proposed to her in the solarium," Esther suggested. "Do we have a solarium?"

"No."

"Then, on second thought, it's probably the other 'S' word. Selfish," Esther said.

"This house has such wonderful bones and it's coming to life right before our eyes," Laura said. "Maybe when Mrs. Childers sees the finished product she'll be glad the house wasn't leveled."

"I don't think anyone is going to change Francesca Childers' views on anything." Esther said. "Image is everything with that woman. Her objection to leaving the house standing could be as simple as not wanting others to know that she once owned a house that became an eyesore. Or, was one before you two waved your magic wands."

"Thanks for the compliments," Russ said, "but we've still got a lot to do here before the clock strikes midnight."

"NINCOMPOOPS," Francesca Childers said to herself. "We've raised an entire generation of nincompoops!"

She often talked to herself. It was better to sound off in the privacy of her own home, then later temper her words when she met with the builders and decorators who were on the Home Owners Association Board or with the officers of the Portland home builders' association.

She debated whether she could sue the whole outfit. After all, a verbal contract held some merit in a courtroom. After much deliberation, she had become convinced legal action wasn't worth the time or the cost involved. She felt betrayed, though. When she sold the land for the Street of Dreams project she had been told that the Childers Estate mansion would be demolished.

"And, that's as it should be," she said once again to herself. Didn't these people recognize that it was important to have a cohesive look throughout the neighborhood? You didn't get as wealthy as her family had without making every decision in life based on the bottom line. The decision to let the old house stand was not only costing her money, it could lower her status in the community.

Her own son failed to recognize that. He was a disappointment in so many ways. Where was his head for business? Had he missed out entirely on that gene?

She walked past the mirrored wall in her elegant dining room and glanced at her reflection, noting that she had been diligent and kept herself in fine form. A size eight at this age, and still able to turn heads. She was strong too.

"Mother would be proud," she said aloud.

Jonathan—who had been styling her hair since it was naturally blonde—had found the perfect geometric lines for her signature haircut. Others took notice when Francesca Childers entered a room. That too was as it should be, she thought.

Francesca was still miffed by the decision to restore the old house when she reclined on the living room couch and fell into a fitful sleep.

The next morning she thought about her family home again, talking to the bathroom mirror this time as she applied her makeup. She'd have to accept that the homebuilders' association wouldn't bend. The Childers' home should have been torn down a few years ago when she had the chance.

Maybe the Howard woman would be overwhelmed with the scope of the project, making all this angst for nothing, Francesca consoled herself.

"If you're tempted to decorate your bedroom like a luxury hotel, rent a suite at The Hilton for the weekend. It comes with maid service."

5

Laura slathered the sunscreen across her upper arms. She hated the slippery lotion, but it was the price she paid for her unusual coloring. Her skin was light and would be tanned to a beautiful Coppertone bronze by the end of summer, but she had to take it slowly. Eight to ten hours a day of sun wasn't a good beauty regime for anyone. If she wanted proof, she could go to the museum and check out the photos of the wrinkled faces of Oregon pioneer women.

She tucked her thick auburn hair behind her ears when she was on the job site, but she had never grown comfortable wearing the required yellow hard hat. Most of her work was inside, away from danger, she insisted.

Russ cautioned her regularly, but she just grinned at him, her green eyes sparkling, and told him to sound the alarm if any safety inspectors stepped onto the property. Russ was a by-the-book guy in every other way, but he knew this was a battle he'd never win.

Unlike many women, Laura wasn't displeased with her appearance, and at 5'8' with a slim, leggy look, she could wear almost any fashion that hit the runway.

"If I wanted to," she said to herself.

Her preferred attire on a mid-summer work site was bright-colored tank tops and jeans or shorts. She accessorized her skinny jeans and top with a warm gray Portland State University sweatshirt on nippy mornings. Her one concession to the building trade was to wear sturdy hard-toed boots to protect herself from injury.

"HOMEOWNERS' ASSOCIATIONS are the work of the Devil," Laura complained. "Do you want to go to this meeting?"

"Sorry," Russ said.

"You don't sound very sorry."

"I'm not the one who was elected to the board."

The initial Homeowners' Association at the Dreams project had been created to have a group that could make sure that landscaping styles, exterior paint colors, and housing styles were compatible so future home buyers would have an appealing neighborhood. The current HOA would be handed over to the new residents as soon as all seven dwellings were sold.

Not a minute too soon for Laura.

The board included Francesca Childers and her son and decorator Jamen, builder Gary Young and his designer Charmaigne White, and Tom and Helen Parker who were building the Tudor-inspired house at the end of the street.

Laura wished she had thought as fast as Russ, who was able to bail out of an appointment to the group when he mentioned that having an uneven number of people on the Board would make it easier to have decisive votes on any issues that might arise.

Charmaigne White, who had recently appeared on a locally televised home décor show, was talking in a loud voice as Laura entered the sales office, a small structure which would later become a social center for the families who lived on the street. Laura had made the error earlier of calling the woman "Char" and was told that the name Charmaigne would soon be a household word for elegant decor. It was not to be shortened.

"The director says the camera just eats me up," Charmaigne said.

It was nice to know that something was getting fed on that film set, Laura thought. Despite the well-applied makeup, Charmaigne's eyes seemed to have taken a step and a half back in her face, making room for the once full cheeks to sink in, emphasizing her high, angular cheekbones. The young woman was a poster child for a Feed Anorexics Today campaign.

Charmaigne was explaining how her own career "simply soared" after she was filmed for several short spots on a fledgling cable station.

"I'd think you'd watch OMG-TV, Laura. It's an easy way for beginners to pick up on sophisticated trends from San Francisco and New York."

Had the woman truly said "OMG-TV?" Laura's face showed her confusion.

"OMG," Charmaigne said, emphasizing each letter. "Oregon Mansions and Gardens."

Laura thanked her for the tip and somehow kept a straight face while finding a chair at the table. Maybe the local station had borrowed its name from the surprised homeowners on HGTV programs who could never think of anything deeper to say than "Oh My God" when they first saw their redecorated homes.

The rain splashed against the windows overlooking what was to become a common area behind the social center. The HOA committee spent the next hour trying to decide whether they would open themselves up to liability if they added a pond behind the structure or if they should use fountains instead.

In Portland. City of Roses. And over 37 inches of rain annually.

Francesca Childers said she "rued the day" that bank financing had allowed young families and their "urchin offspring" to buy in an upscale neighborhood that had at one time been the grounds of a grand Italianate home of Portland's past. She tried to persuade the other building teams to choose real estate agents who would be discreet in selecting only adults "of stature in the community" to view the properties.

Esther, who had offered to bring refreshments, sneaked in the back door by the compact kitchen. She opened her mouth to protest what Mrs. Childers' had just said, but Laura signaled her to zip it. Laura wanted to hear how far Francesca Childers would go in wanting to select the owners.

There were a few more carefully veiled statements by Mrs. Childers, pointing out that there were no public schools available in the area and "surely only those who could afford to have children transported daily to a private academy" should be considered as potential buyers.

At the end of Francesca's oration, Mrs. Parker timidly called for a vote on the original question of pond vs. fountain.

With the feds, banks and credit unions now tightening lending policies, Laura doubted that anyone with small children could afford to buy a home in the newly-created luxury neighborhood. She sided with those who favored fountains for safety anyway. Hers was a vote to put the Childers woman in her place.

"Why else have secret ballots?" she thought.

Laura supposed she should have expected today's discussion after what she sat through at the first meeting of the HOA board. There had been half a dozen items on the prepared agenda, but the group had spent over two hours discussing Mrs. Childers' proposal that there be a theme for the neighborhood and each house have at least one room decorated to address that theme.

The discussion had ended just short of a cat fight between Mrs. Childers and Charmaigne who had initially agreed, but dared to suggest FantasyLand as the theme of choice instead of Mrs. Childers' Portlandia vision.

Worse than the meetings, Laura thought, was the social time set aside at the end of each session. She had never felt the need to bond with co-workers when she could use the time to get some work done instead.

She'd heard tales about "condo commandos" in planned unit developments, but this was her first up-close-and-personal experience with a home owners' association.

Esther came into the room quietly.

"Serve to the left with left hand, retrieve from the right," Esther repeated to herself. She moved toward the table, reminding herself to place Francesca Childers' plate on the table first.

Mrs. Childers had returned to the discussion of her idea for a theme for the homes, but had now progressed to suggesting a "Portlandia room" in each house. Laura thought it was bad enough that the new homes would each eventually have a name on the literature from the sales office. If she kept wasting time with this group, the Graham Construction project would be called Unfinished Symphony.

Esther smiled sweetly as she walked up behind Francesca, leaned forward, and tilted the dessert plate slightly. The strawberry shortcake slid off the plate. It landed on the left shoulder of the ivory sheath dress and traveled down the front, the red strawberry syrup splashing on Francesca Childers' dress and the cake coming to rest on the woman's lap. Esther still held the plate aloft.

"Look what you've done!" Francesca shrieked.

"I'm sorry," Esther said.

"You're *sorry?* That's your response? *You're sorry?*"

"I'd be happy to pay your cleaning bill."

"This is Armani's."

"I didn't know you'd borrowed it. Please tell Armani I'll pay for the cleaning."

"You low class idiot!"

"I may be an idiot, but I don't borrow clothes," Esther said.

Jamen reached for his mother's arm and the woman pushed his hand aside.

"If we head home quickly, I think I can get the stain out for you, Mother," he said.

"And, now I've got a son who thinks he's Heloise."

Jamen ignored the remark, helped his mother out of her chair, and showed her to the door.

"Thank you, Mrs. Graham, for the lovely treats," Jamen said. "It was a dear, dear gesture," he added as he guided his mother toward the door.

"How many times have I told you not to call me 'Mother?'" she asked him as the door closed.

There was no comment from anyone else at the table as Esther distributed the desserts. The discussion of themes ended abruptly without a decision. As folks drifted off, Laura turned toward Esther.

"About Francesca," she said. "I thought we both decided to take the high road."

"We did."

"And?" Laura asked.

"I took an off ramp by mistake."

ESTHER GRAHAM SELDOM went to the building site when neither of the other two partners was there. She had forgotten her sun hat and she wanted to retrieve it before the start of the neighborhood kids' parade that would march past on the sidewalk in front of Graham Construction today. The annual procession was not elaborate, but the kids worked for days ahead of time decorating their bicycles and making costumes for the family pets.

Today promised to be unseasonably warm, but she thought she and Hammer could scoot over to the Dreams place before nine, claim the hat, and get back in less than thirty minutes.

Esther gave a single sharp whistle and Hammer took the porch steps two at a time and joined her as she entered the old house. He started to growl immediately. Then, two sharp barks.

"You can hit the hydrant on the way out," Esther told him. "We'll just be a minute here while I get my hat."

Hammer ran toward the kitchen and Esther heard a man's voice.

"Call your damn dog off."

"Not until you tell me why you're on private property," Esther demanded. She still hadn't seen the person who was speaking.

"Hammer, let him through," she said. The dog whined, but moved aside. Esther looped her thumb through the dog's collar.

The short dark-haired man who stepped through the door was dressed more like a sales clerk than a construction worker. She knew she hadn't seen this person on the Street of Dreams before.

"Tell me what you're doing here," she said, "or I let the dog loose."

"Here's the deal," he said. The tone of his voice made Esther think that he was making up this story as he went along. "There's been some suspicious activity out here and I was making sure nobody was wandering the construction sites at night and stealing from you folks."

"Not buying," Esther said. She reached in her purse for a small aerosol container.

"What's that?"

"Pepper spray," she said. "And you have sixty seconds to get out of here." She took the cap off the container and pointed the nozzle on the can toward him.

"Call the dog off," he said. "I'll go out the front way."

"The dog stays," she said with the nozzle of the spray can aimed at eye level. "Turn around, lift that window and step out. It's only about a four foot drop."

"Look. Just let me explain."

"110 NRD," was her only response.

"Huh?"

"I memorized the Oregon license plate number when I saw a vehicle I didn't recognize parked near here."

"You can't do that."

"Just did."

Hammer growled more menacingly and Esther waved the canister toward the intruder.

She heard the man swear as his feet hit the ground after he went out the window. She stuck her arm out the window, pushed the plastic button on top of the can, and sprayed his fleeing back.

"Good dog," she praised Hammer. "Let's find my hat and get out of here."

She borrowed Charmaigne's phone at the site next door so she could tell Laura that there had been an intruder.

"Why didn't you call the police?" Laura asked.

"School's out. It's summer vacation," Esther said. "They're going to be dealing with family disturbances, illegal fireworks calls, and college-age drunks all week. I thought I'd give them a break." And, I don't have a cell phone, she thought to herself.

"Did you get a good description of the guy?" Laura asked.

"Hammer and I would remember him if we saw him again. He was a sleaze ball."

Laura opened her mouth to speak, but then closed it. There was no appropriate response to that.

"We took care of it with this," Esther told Laura later that afternoon while holding up the aerosol can.

"You two carry pepper spray?"

"Hair spray," Esther corrected. "That little sucker left looking better than when he arrived."

"Hide bottle caps filled with PineSol inside high kitchen cupboards. The aroma makes others think you've been cleaning instead of reading a mystery and eating chocolate all day."

6

Francesca Childers had been widowed for over twenty years, but the venom she felt for her late husband had, if anything, increased with each year since his death. She hoped he and The Slut had met again and linked up in a torrid relationship. In Hell.

She wondered now if she'd had doubts about the man even before their lovely summer garden nuptials all those years ago. Thank God she'd kept her maiden name. There had never been any debate about that. "Childers" was synonymous with wealth, charm and charity in this town. There was no way she would have allowed herself to be addressed as Mrs. William Jones.

She and Bill Jones had been married less than a year when she became suspicious of all those trips he said he was making to play other golf courses in the area. They belonged to the country club. Why would he be traveling to inferior greens?

She might have been able to overlook his dalliances if he hadn't been stupid and gotten the young woman in, as they said in Francesca's youth, "a family way." The Slut was pregnant less than three months after the two linked up.

Just when Francesca thought nothing more could smear her husband's reputation—and even taint the Childers name—The Slut died in what were first thought to be unsavory circumstances. It left the infant no other relatives but Bill Jones. The death raised questions in the community, but the police eventually listed the cause of death as "accidental self-inflicted wounds."

Francesca was distraught, but she received good advice from her mother and her aunt concerning the "unfortunate situation." Yes, those two knew society and the ins and outs of handling scandal. Their advice had shocked her initially, but it had been right on the mark.

Francesca and her husband adopted the little bastard. Her only requirement was that the baby be given the Childers' name. And, he was rechristened with appropriate first and middle names. Jamen Winthrop Childers.

Instead of enduring the snubs of the social elite, Francesca was now viewed as that ultra-modern, understanding young wife who had enough love in her heart to take in the baby. She had raised him as a son and no one had ever mentioned within her hearing that dreadful time when her husband had bedded The Slut.

JAMEN CHILDERS STOPPED by the Graham Construction building site early the next week. He was distributing lavender pieces of paper with script printing announcing an emergency HOA meeting for all builders, designers, decorators, and subcontractors. Anyone who would be on the site during the next months was to gather at 5 p.m. Friday at the social center. The scheduled meeting was set for the precise time when all the crews would be trying to tie down things for the weekend and get out of there. They were not amused.

Jamen was a hard guy for Esther to read. On the one hand he was a highly artistic, skilled decorator. On the other, he seemed to distance himself from the rest of them.

"That's easy," Laura said. "He's embarrassed by his mother."

"Could be, but I think there may be something more there," Esther said. "One minute he comes off as the up-and-coming next best thing in decorators. All masculine and sexy," she added. "The next time I see him, he's standoffish and secretive about his work."

"Maybe he's had people steal his creative ideas in the past," Laura suggested.

"Possible. But, I think he acts more like he's got something to hide."

"And I think you think too much," Laura said. "He's a lovely Mama's boy who has more money than the rest of us to bring his decorating fantasies to life. Frankly, I enjoy his company more than that of the other decorators and designers who prance around here."

"Intentional choice of verbs there?"

"No. But, I have noticed that the only time Jamen's conversation goes over the top is when Mommy Dearest is within earshot," Laura said. "Most men wouldn't suggest a 'lovely rich silk brocade poof for the crowning touch in the foyer.'"

"So you picked up on that one too," Esther said.

"Hit me like a feather boa."

"And, none of this is any of our business," Esther stated firmly

"Then, why did you bring it up?" Laura asked. "You're not homophobic, are you?"

"I can't even spell it," Esther said. "No. Definitely not. There's just something off there. Remember, you heard it here first."

Jamen Childers looked like he had stepped off the page of a JCrew catalog in time to make his daily gym and tanning booth appointments. It was a nice look. He was blonde and blue-eyed and wore the same intentional beard stubble every day. Laura thought he was the direct opposite of Russ, but extremely attractive in his own way.

Laura had known Russ long enough that she sometimes forgot what a great first impression he made when he was introduced to folks. "Folks, nothing," she thought. "It was mostly women who were awestruck."

They might have expected a contractor to be tall and brawny with well-developed upper arms. And, a year-round tan came with the territory. Russ, though, had the most engaging manner. When he smiled, laugh lines framed his twinkly blue eyes.

"That smile unfolded slowly, then smacked you silly with its warmth," she recalled.

Instead of looking scalped, his summertime haircut made him look younger than his thirty-something years. Laura hated it when his dark curls landed on the barber shop floor, but she knew they'd be back in the fall, peeking slyly around his ears.

If Jamen Childers had fallen off the JCrew catalog page, Russell Graham had slipped out early from the cover shoot for an Eddie Bauer publication.

THERE WEREN'T ENOUGH folding chairs to go around Friday afternoon, so several of the subcontractors lined the walls of the meeting room.

It was the end of a long week and Laura was sure she wasn't the only one who resented a meeting called for late Friday afternoon. "Most of these guys would usually have been lifting a second or third beer by this time on a Friday evening," she thought.

Laura squirmed in her chair, trying to get comfortable. She said a silent prayer that the social center would eventually be furnished with more comfortable chairs.

"Let's get this show on the road," Esther said quietly to Russ and Laura. "Any hints about what's going on here?"

Neither responded.

"I recognize the guy in the 1980s suit jacket," Esther said a little too loudly.

Russ shook his head and Laura scoured the room for the coat. It would have been easier to spot if the man's belly hadn't been hanging out, forcing the front of the jacket wide apart.

The president of the builders' association stepped forward and the conversations in the room came to a halt.

Esther was trying to whisper something to Laura from two seating rows over. Laura could neither hear her nor read her lips. Esther tried several times more until the speaker sent her a stern look.

Laura mouthed "later." Esther settled back to listen, but was now glaring at the man who was about to be introduced to the group.

"Thanks for coming," the association president said. "I'm going to make this brief."

"Yeah, right," Esther thought.

"With all the bad publicity this project has been getting, we're concerned about the potential impact on the profit margin for the association. Lately, the only news out of here comes to future home buyers from the Police Bureau.

"*The Oregonian* newsroom employees may claim to be short-staffed, but they're definitely scanning the police log. The stories about this year's Street of Dreams haven't left the up-scale impression we're all shooting for."

"Ahem," the newcomer interrupted. "Let's not say 'shooting.'"

"You guys make your money on the houses," the president continued. "The association makes money on the 'gate.' How many young families do you think are eagerly waiting to drag their preschoolers out to a murder site for a Sunday afternoon open house?"

"It's not that bad," someone said from the back of the room.

"Would you like your profit margin to dip by 20 to 25 percent?" the speaker asked. "What the association doesn't make at this event will have to be made up with a jump in annual dues."

There was a grumble around the room.

"We can't do anything about recent events, but we have a viable plan for damage control," the president said. "We think we can implement it immediately and turn the publicity around overnight."

They were all listening now.

"We've hired a spokesperson and publicist for the Street of Dreams. His will be the only voice talking to the press from now on," he added. "We don't usually put someone on salary until it's time to promote the August opening, but this year has obviously been different—and disastrous from a public relations point of view.

"Edward, step forward," he said to Mr. Eighty's Suit. "This, gentlemen, is Edward Simmons and he's going to save our collective bacon."

Laura bristled. The women had been off-handedly left out of the discussion. (Only gentlemen need apply.) She clenched her teeth and sat quietly.

Esther leaned back and asked in a stage whisper "Is 'collective bacon' a euphemism for 'fat asses'?"

Russ shushed her.

Edward Simmons explained that he'd be at the site off and on 24 hours a day from now until the project was finished. He'd also be a night watchman of sorts while he was there after 5 p.m.

"I want you to give Simmons full access to the site and answer any questions he has," the president said. "His first suggestion—and it's one I wish I had thought of—is that we provide you all with hanging name badges so we can spot if an intruder is on site."

The earlier grumble was replaced with a group guffaw.

"Yeah, like that's going to happen," Laura heard someone say. "It will be a zillion degrees out here this summer, blazing sun, and the roofers are going to put on necklaces."

"The damn things are safety hazards," another worker said.

"There's no discussion. Having Ed here . . . "

"I go by Ward," Simmons interrupted.

"Having Ward here as an additional set of eyes could prevent another tragedy and more bad press."

It was obvious which was more important to the man.

"Those of you who want to stay and get acquainted with Ward are welcome to," the president continued. "I know some of you have places to be."

The room emptied, leaving the president and his new hire with no one to talk to but each other.

"THAT'S HIM!" Esther said the minute she, Laura and Russ were out the door. "Mr. Simmons has slicked his hair back and borrowed a store mannequin's suit, but he's the guy who was inside our house the other morning."

"Are you sure?"

"Do you honestly think God would have created a second after he saw that one?" she asked.

"Did you ask him if he was with the homebuilders group when you met him the other morning?" Russ asked.

"I didn't have to ask. Hammer had already signaled that the guy wasn't legit," Esther said.

"Maybe Simmons was checking out the job before he accepted it."

"More like he cased the joint, then sought the job," said an unconvinced Esther.

"Surely the association would have run a criminal history check on a potential employee with this level of responsibility," Laura said.

"Has it occurred to anybody on this planet but me," Esther asked, "that a criminal history check is only accurate for sixty seconds after it's completed?"

"You two obviously took an instant dislike to Simmons," Russ said, "but we could use a night watchman around here."

"Not him," Laura said.

"Aren't you jumping to judgment here?"

"He has dark beady eyes," Esther answered.

"Dyed hair, slicked back with Crisco," Laura added.

"You've only known the guy for ten minutes," Russ protested.

"He has hair on the back of his fingers," Esther added.

"And no chin," Laura put in. "He reeks of dishonesty."

Russ shook his head. He'd never understand these two. "Well, as long as you gave him a fair chance. I'd hate to have you rush to any hasty opinions."

"He's a snake," Esther summarized.

"WHAT DO URBAN chickens eat?" Esther asked on the way home from the Friday meeting.

"Tofu?" suggested Laura.

"I'm serious here," Esther said. "I'm thinking of keeping some chickens on the roof-top garden at my place." Russ had converted the storage rooms over the carpenter's shop at Graham Construction into an efficiency apartment for Esther. The unit had French doors to a charming roof garden.

"May I be so brave as to ask why you're considering chickens," Laura said.

"For omelets, of course," Esther answered. "Or, drumsticks if they get defiant."

Laura rolled her eyes. Esther had apparently discovered the "Keep Portland Weird" stickers that had sprouted on the bumpers of thousands of cars and luxury SUVs around town. Raising so-called urban chickens would be a logical next step for Esther as she continued to adjust to Portland.

Laura suspected Portland had more neon-lit sushi bars, shared granola recipes, and programs for recycling waste food than any other town in the country. All this, she noted, in a city where plastic shopping bags were banned.

The only thing stranger than the bumper sticker itself, Laura thought, was that Portlanders swiped the slogan from one used in Austin, Texas. "How about using 'Keep Portland Honest,'" she wondered.

"I'm afraid you're out of luck on the chicken front," Russ said. "The neighborhood isn't zoned for raising chickens."

"Rats!"

55

"Not rats either," he added.

"You could grow more herbs," Laura suggested. "But be careful what kind of leaves are on those plants." Unlike their neighbors in Washington State, across the Columbia River from Portland, voters had surprised many in Oregon by turning down a measure to legalize marijuana.

Esther was deep in thought and didn't hear the gardening suggestion. She had spent all morning thinking of fowl names for her future flock. All for naught.

"First plastic bags. Now chickens," she muttered. "What's next?"

"If you're too chicken to use a bright color for an accent wall, start with pillows and a throw in that hue."

7

Laura woke with a start, throwing back the covers and propelling Louise off the bed.

"What was that?" she asked the cat. Louise meowed once, but didn't answer the question.

They both cowered as the noise started again. It sounded like a miniature machine gun firing right at the house. She ticked off the possible causes. Not electrical. It didn't sound like plumbing. It wasn't a leaking roof.

She'd call Russ.

"Can you come down here? I need you," she said into the phone receiver.

"It's six in the morning," he said in a groggy voice. "Which coast are you calling from?" He hung up, and Laura assumed he rolled over to go back to sleep

Laura dialed the number again.

"Please don't hang up," she yelled. "This is Laura and it sounds like The Harrington is under attack."

"Are you dreaming?"

"Louise and I are both wide awake. There's a Gawd awful noise, like continual pounding coming from above us," she said. "Can you at least look up the block and see if there's somebody on the roof."

"I'm on it."

"The roof?"

"I'm coming down to your house," he corrected as he reached for a sweatshirt. Laura wasn't overly dramatic as a rule, so what was going on?

He jogged up the block and the front door of Laura's house flew open before he could knock.

"Come up to the bedroom with me," she said.

"Nice start, Babe."

"This is serious. We need you to hear something. I've never heard anything like it before in my life. And, it's scaring Louise."

He scooped up Louise, a male cat with gender issues, and followed Laura up the stairs to the bedroom. The room was absolutely quiet.

"Just wait," Laura said.

The room stayed silent.

"We did not imagine this," she said, looking toward the cat for confirmation. The cat had climbed inside Russ' faded navy blue sweatshirt and was settling in under his elbow. Louise still felt some allegiance to

Russ, who had rescued the abandoned kitten at a past building site.

Laura paced.

The room seemed to grow quieter.

"Call me if you hear it again," Russ said, "unless you're inviting me to stay in your bedroom all day."

"That call was an SOS signal, not an invitation," she said. She waited, hoping the noise would occur again. It had been loud and persistent.

"This is like when I take the truck in to the garage and the engine won't make the canary noise for the mechanic," Laura said.

"Is something wrong with the truck? I could look at that while I'm down here."

"No, thanks. This was a rat-tat-tat-tat drilling noise. In the house," she insisted.

The noise started again, louder than before. It sounded like a machine gun firing in the attic. Laura and Louise jumped and Russ shook his head.

"You've got a flicker," he said. "A bird. And he's feeling horny."

"Russ!"

"Flickers are part of the woodpecker species and they drum like that to broadcast their territory and to attract a mate. If the drumming is on wood, they're trying to excavate a nest," he added. "Since this one's drilling on the metal flashing around the chimney, I'd say he's putting out an 'all call' for a girlfriend. As long as he sticks to the metal, he won't do any structural damage."

"So what do I do?"

"Nothing. He'll be gone after nesting season," Russ said. "Get the binoculars."

"I am not—did you hear not?—spying on copulating wildlife."

"These guys are quite common in Oregon. Beautiful birds, about a foot long. They're brown with a buff-colored breast with black dots. They have red coloring under the wings and tail along with a black necklace." He hesitated. "But that's probably just for dress occasions," he added. "You can tell the males because they have a red mustache near their bill."

The noise sounded again, this time longer and more ear-piercing than before.

"See! It sounds like shots," Laura said.

"Relax, you two. The guy's looking for a prom date."

Laura thanked Russ for coming down, and offered him a cup of coffee. He turned her down so he could go back up the block, shower, and officially start the day.

Laura assured Louise that the noise wasn't perilous and, since they had no choice that they would have a feathered addition to the family for as long as it wanted to stay. They christened the flicker Fletcher.

HAMMER STROLLED through the living room area in Esther's small quarters. The dog often came calling when Russ was out on a job. He found Esther lying on the floor. Hammer eyed her warily, then stood next to her, reached over to lick her right ear, and finally flopped down by her side.

"That is not the 'downward facing dog' position," Esther told him. She had only attended two yoga sessions so far, but she was also sure she hadn't heard anything about slobbering on the person on the floor mat next to you. Esther righted herself with some difficulty and consulted the printed sheet showing yoga poses for the beginner.

She had signed up for the class at the YMCA after taking a break from her marathon of reducing diets. Since none of the diets seemed to work anyway, she thought, as she dipped her spoon into the Tollhouse chocolate chip cookie dough, her new plan was to concentrate on flexibility, endurance and sense of balance.

She thought the yoga instructor had mentioned "less stress and more spirituality" also, but the young woman was not a native English speaker, and it was hard for Esther to hear while balancing in Warrior I position. Then, the teacher had dared to give them all homework. She asked each student to think of a "mantra," a word or phrase to be repeated silently to bring relaxation as they started each yoga session.

Esther thought this was worse than having to select and remember computer passwords. She had solved the computer problem by consistently using the password "incorrect." If she forgot her password, the computer screen would tip her that "the password is incorrect." It might be an old joke, but it worked for her.

Following the same logic, she chose "I-got-nothin'" as her mantra. That decided, she returned to the bowl of cookie dough.

New yogi Esther may have thought she needed to tone up, but to the outside world the older woman was in incredible shape.

"It's because she runs everywhere she goes," Laura had explained to Russ. "She never sits still for more than five minutes, and I think she uses those minutes to think about where she's going to trot off to next. There's more energy in her 5'2" frame than in the two of us put together."

"She does kind of hustle, doesn't she?" Russ asked.

"Hustle? The woman needs derailment insurance."

"Do you know she's hitting seventy? With Aunt Esther, I never think about her age," Russ said.

"That's because she always has on bright colors. Don't worry if you see a coral flash, it's just Esther returning from Macy's," Laura said. "And her hair may have grayed some, but it looks like the new highlighting trend that younger women are doing now. They're paying big bucks for that look, and Esther wakes up, runs a 97-cent comb through her hair, and looks every bit as good."

"Exactly," Russ said.

"Did Esther ever live in New Mexico?"

"No, but I know why you ask. She bought all that silver and turquoise jewelry she wears when she was in her genealogy phase. She thought she'd found her American Indian heritage. It turned out to be a typo on the family tree."

"Seeing her clear, azure blue eyes in the mirror didn't give her a clue that something might be wrong?" Laura asked.

"I'll tell you one thing. Aunt Essie absolutely saved my backside when she took over the business end of the company for me. I had invoices stacked all over the place. I'd lose track of which subcontractors I'd already paid. It was a mess. The company was bleeding money," he confessed.

"So you hired an emergency room nurse?"

"Something like that."

LAURA ARRIVED AT the work site and found Russ on the second floor landing, where he was shimmying a car jack under a two-by-four to temporarily hold a header in place while he widened the door opening to meet modern building code standards. He was obviously preoccupied, and appeared to have confused car tools with construction ones, Laura thought. She charged ahead anyway, thinking what was on her mind was equally as important as Russ' current balancing act.

"I know it's 'out of sequence,' or whatever that phrase is you use when I want to do something before it's scheduled. But I need to have locking exits on this house," Laura said. "Today!"

"Whoa!"

Laura hated it when Russ did that. His "whoa" may have meant "slow down" to him, but to her it was the same as if he'd put his palm out in front of her face.

"Don't 'whoa' me!"

"OK."

"It's hot. It's supposed to be over 80 degrees today, according to Rhonda, and . . ."

"Who's Rhonda?"

"The TV weather lady."

"So it's hot," Russ said to get Laura back on track.

"And, right before noon, I was up on the top rung of the ladder in my shorts. . ."

"Not the red shorts," Russ said.

"What difference does it make what color they are? My point is that Wart waltzed in here and called up to me to ask if I'm wearing my ID tag."

"From below?" Russ asked.

"Yes, from below." she yelled.

"In the red shorts."

Laura was beside herself. She didn't know quite what that meant, but she knew she was mad enough for two people.

"I've told you Wart is a pervert," she said.

"It's Ward."

"Who cares? He creeps me out. Esther, too."

"You'll have locks and dead bolts on the doors by noon tomorrow," Russ said, returning to his current task.

"Thank you."

"Found furniture is fun to restore, but it doesn't qualify as 'found' if you lift it from your neighbor's porch."

8

Reading the obituaries in *The Oregonian* had become part of Laura's morning routine. Brush her teeth. Feed Louise. Read the obits.

Some might have thought her reading habits odd, but Laura found it comforting to know others shared the experience of losing a spouse. She didn't feel like the only widow in the world.

"Have you ever noticed they die in alphabetical order?" Esther asked.

Laura chose not to answer.

It had been two years since Todd Howard's death and Laura was making good progress. She no longer thought of him daily and sometimes—well, a few selected times—she remembered the good times they'd had together instead of dwelling on the others.

"YOU'RE SURE QUIET today," Laura said to Russ during their morning coffee and snack break. "Is there something I need to know about this project?"

"No," Russ said. "We're actually in better shape than I thought we'd be on the remodel. I don't envy the guys trying to meet the deadline with new construction. They've got a fairly tight timeline."

"Are you mad at me?" she asked.

"I think I'm mad at me," he said. "Do you ever wonder if you ought to be doing more with your life? I like what we're doing," he said. "And, I love who I'm doing it with," he added, throwing a piece of popcorn across the table at her.

She caught it and threw it back at him. Maybe it was their maturity level that had him worried, she thought.

"Isn't it a little early for a mid-life crisis?" Laura asked.

"Hey, I'm on the lean side of 40," he said.

"Very lean, I might point out."

"Thank you," he said. "I have an aunt and a girlfriend who keep me hopping. It beats going to the gym." He hesitated, then added "I like our work, and I like that I can get away on weekends," he said. "I'm happy and healthy . . ."

"And you sound like you're in a TV spot for Geritol," Laura said. "What gives?"

"It seems like I should be contributing more to life," he said. "I've been watching the coverage of the flood back East for weeks, and I can't get those victims out of my mind. They were probably happy with their homes and jobs, too, and now they've got nothing to show for any of that hard work."

"I'm not making light of the situation," she said, "but I think that's why they call it a disaster."

"Nicely summarized," he said. "It still seems like we should be able to help." He let the subject drop, but Laura knew she hadn't heard the last of it.

"YOU LOOK GLUM," Esther said.

"How would you feel if you were my age and discovered that you can't keep a man?"

"That's nonsense," Esther answered.

"Russ is leaving for the East Coast this morning."

"Yes."

"And I thought I was going with him."

"And. . ." Esther said.

"Then he said it was something he needed to do alone. He said the last thing they need back there during the hurricane cleanup is an interior decorator."

"He's right, you know. They're more into basic needs back there. Roofs, heat, water, fresh food . . ."

"I get it," Laura said. "I'm not stupid. But then he said I should get out and see other people while he's gone."

Esther looked uncomfortable.

"You knew about this, didn't you?" Laura asked.

"You and I both knew about it," Esther said. "He's been talking about volunteering back there for weeks.

He's a good carpenter and they could use him. Him and another 5,003 like him," she added.

"But I thought he was talking about the team going," Laura said. "All of us at Graham Construction."

"I think he was originally," Esther said. "But then he took a look at how rough the job is back there and decided it would be less complicated if he just hopped a plane, showed up, and offered his skills."

"So we don't matter."

"You matter, Laura," Esther answered. "Russ is a good guy, but he's traditional. He thinks he's keeping you safe."

"By leaving me here with Concrete Man and Wart?"

RUSS CLIMBED INTO the passenger seat of Laura's truck. She didn't glance at him as she put the truck in gear to take him and his duffle bag to Portland International. Both Russ and Laura were silent on the ride out to PDX.

He knew working on a construction crew in the aftermath of a flood wouldn't be safe for Laura. And, now he feared that she wouldn't be safe in Oregon, either. It was a no-win situation for him. Neither decision was perfect. He had finally flipped a coin. Four times. But tails kept coming up. That's when he decided to fly to New Jersey alone, but for a shorter stint than he had planned originally.

Russ was quiet, re-thinking his decision. His volunteer weeks on the East Coast would be for "the greater good" he told himself for the umpteenth time. Laura had police protection in Portland. He wouldn't be gone all that long. Three or four weeks at most. What was her problem?

The only exchanges en route to the airport were occasional gasps as one or the other of them realized that traffic was coming to a halt for no apparent reason. Regular commuters on I-205 understood this strange phenomenon, but she thought the engineers who designed this strip of Oregon freeway should have been condemned to drive the road for all eternity. Laura took the 24A off ramp and headed toward the airport.

The management at PDX had already done everything in its power to prevent long romantic goodbyes. There was no more waiting for the plane together, no exchanging a lingering hug and kiss, and definitely no running to board the plane at the last minute.

As she eased the truck up to the curb, Laura got a defiant look in her eyes, took the keys out of the ignition, and raced around the back of the truck. Russ put his bag on the pavement and pulled her into his arms.

"I won't be gone long," he said. "I promise."

"You promised me it wouldn't rain today too," she said between kisses.

"I'm a better builder than a forecaster."

She wished she could see into the future to know that he would come back to her. Wasn't charity supposed to begin at home? Couldn't he volunteer somewhere on the West Coast?

Russ hugged her one last time, wiped a tear from her cheek, and turned to go through the door that led to the escalator that would deliver him to the airline check-in counters.

NEITHER THE ELECTRONIC turn signal on the truck nor her hand waving out the window in the rain could get Laura over to the correct lane to exit the airport. She wound up following the horseshoe-shaped road past the terminal a second time. She missed her single chance to change lanes safely that time too and gallantly started around to the left for a third try. At least this wasn't as bad as the time she forgot which level she had parked on in the parking structure.

On the third try, she exited successfully. She looked to her right and saw the tall blue and yellow sign that spelled out her four favorite letters: I. K. E. A.

"Love those Swedish flag colors," she said to herself. She flipped up the turn signal indicator, glanced briefly behind her, and pulled right across three lanes of traffic in one swoop, oblivious to the sounds of screeching brakes and blowing horns.

"Sometimes you have to do what you have to do," she thought. And, right now, she had to check out geometric print pillows for accessories in the future family room at the Dreams home.

Too bad IKEA sales staff didn't work on commission, Laura thought as she wandered from one display roomette to the next. She could be a big help to them today

By the time she reached the cash register, she had selected two area rugs for the project house (plus a smaller one for the sunroom at The Harrington.) The color schemes for these rooms had been mapped in her head since the project started. Now, she was executing the plan, making sure that the selected rugs would help the colors flow smoothly from one room to the next.

There was no use wasting a good IKEA stop, so she also picked up new bedding for her upstairs bedroom at The Harrington. Some women her age were shoe addicts. Laura craved fresh, crisp bed linens and pillow shams.

An IKEA employee helped her unload the purchases from two shopping carts and put them into the truck bed. Laura checked to see that she had enough cash left for a McMeal on the way home, and turned the key in the ignition.

SHE SAW FLASHING red and blue lights reflecting in the rear-view mirror. Laura pulled to the right to let an ambulance go by, but the lights kept flashing. It took another thirty seconds before she realized that a cop car—not an ambulance—had pulled in right behind her. Crap. Was there anything else that could go wrong this week?

"Could I see your license please, Ma'am?"

"I'm not a 'ma'am,'" she said under her breath as she dug out the license.

"I beg your pardon."

"My Aunt Maude was a 'ma'am,'" she said.

"Your license, please?"

"My grandmother was a ma'am. Do I look like a 'ma'am'?"

"Now, look lady. . ."

She handed him the Oregon driver's license with her thumb over the photo. She was only a few blocks from home. What was his problem?

"You ran a red light back there."

"It was orange."

"Orange?" he asked with a wanna-bet challenge in his eyes.

"Orange." She'd have said something more clever, but nothing rhymes with orange. "It was yellow and then it turned red. Red and yellow. Orange."

He shook his head slowly.

"It turned yellow right as I got there," she explained. "If I'd slammed on my brakes, the idiot behind me would have landed in my truck bed."

"I was the idiot behind you."

"I rest my case."

"Are you always this hostile?" he asked. His tone sounded almost caring and there was no "ma'am" at the end of the sentence. And, he had nice eyes.

"Look, I've had a hell-eck," she corrected herself, "of a week. I found a body, and my boyfriend left. I forgot to eat breakfast, and now you."

Laura knew she was babbling. She never cried in public. Until today.

"I'm going to write this up as a warning," he said.

"Thank you," she said with a hiccup.

Double damn! Damn he was cute. And, damn she couldn't stop crying

"How far are you headed?"

"Home. Another half mile in."

"Get your purse and get out of the car. I'm taking you in," he said.

"You're arresting me?"

"No, I'm taking you home. You're in no condition to drive." He walked back to the cruiser to call in his destination. He reported it as a "welfare check."

She didn't argue. He was probably right. The tears had turned into quiet sobs and now there were twice as many hiccups.

Laura wasn't about to leave her IKEA haul in her truck. The cop patiently helped move the rolled rugs and other merchandise to the back seat of the patrol car, the rugs gently bent to extend up the back seat windows. This was clearly against procedure, but it was going to be only a two or three block run.

Laura got in the front seat, carefully buckling the seat belt before the officer drove the few blocks to The Harrington.

"Wait on the porch while I go in," he said as he reached for her house keys. "I'm going to check the place."

She ignored his instructions and stepped into the entryway to wait. After all, it was her house.

"Sit," he commanded as he steered her toward the couch when he came back downstairs. She melted into the sofa. She could hear him stumbling around in her kitchen. The microwave buzzed and he brought her a cup of hot tea. "Sweet," she thought.

"Don't forget to pick up your vehicle in the morning," he said as he handed her the keys and headed for the door. "And no more red lights."

"Orange," she countered.

"Earth tones never go out of style. Add zest to a room with orange accessories."

9

Each raindrop bounced twice on the hood of Esther's rig as she drove toward the Dreams site with Laura riding shotgun. The uneven pattern of the splatting raindrops sounded like practice for the percussion section in a middle school band class. Laura and Esther had decided to travel back and forth to the Dream site together as neither of them was comfortable being there alone. Esther had packed up the laptop computer, her paperwork and the end-of-the-month payroll info to bring with her. The weather was not unusual for Oregon. There was a long-standing tradition of beautiful days the third week in May in Portland, followed by record rains for Memorial Day weekend. Congress could move the observance of Memorial Day to any date they chose. Oregon would have rain that day and sporadically until early July.

The two women held the umbrella over the computer equipment and walked toward the side door where they had parked Esther's boxy Honda Element. They both stepped forward to be under the overhang on the side porch. Laura tried the key three times, but the door didn't open. She handed Esther the key ring and took the umbrella to try to cover Esther and the equipment while the other woman tried the key.

No go.

Esther leaned her head against the door to listen for any activity inside.

"Do you hear whistling?" she asked Laura.

"No."

"I smell Italian spices," Esther said.

"I think the Italianate house is influencing your sense of smell."

"Maybe, but somebody's in there and they're cooking something that smells like spaghetti sauce." Esther took another whiff, and knocked on the door. She was eagerly inhaling what she now suspected was the aroma of lasagna when the whistling stopped. The women could hear heavy footsteps coming across the old hardwood floors toward the door.

"I don't like this," Laura said.

"I've got your back—until your nose bleeds."

"I'll remember that."

"You block. I'll follow," Esther said, but it was too late. The door swung open.

"I wasn't expecting you this early," an older man said. He had weathered tanned skin and a friendly smile— neither of which told the women who he was and why he was inside what was supposed to be a secure construction site.

"Don't stand out there in the rain," he said. "We'll do introductions when you get inside. I hope you don't mind, but I brought my coffee pot and my own lunch for later." Whoever he was, he was obviously making himself right at home, Laura thought. A harvest gold 1970s coffee percolator and a miniature-size crock pot from the same era sat on the floor near one of the few live wall outlets.

"Before I forget," he said, "here are your new keys to the exterior doors. I had one made for each of us and one for Russ when he returns. The extra one is to keep at Graham Construction. I didn't know how many you'd need and there was a price break if we bought five."

Laura wanted to ask "what's this 'we,' stuff?" Instead, she held out her hand for one of the keys.

"You ladies are either the quiet types or you're a little stunned," he said. "Please tell me that Russell remembered to tell you that he hired me to be on site while he's gone. I've got a 'honey do' list a mile long of things he wants me to complete before he gets back." He waved a list typed on Graham Construction Company letterhead toward them. "My specialty is laying tile. All of the Gallo boys worked beside my Dad learning that. And, I'm a darn good paper hanger."

Laura sincerely hoped that he was referring to wallpaper and not bad checks.

"Plus, Russell was clear that my main job is to look out for you ladies' safety."

"That answers why you're here . . ." Esther said.

". . . but he didn't say a word about any of this to us," Laura finished.

"Oh, I forgot something," he said as he handed Esther his hire notice and a federal W-4 form that he had filled out. "I'm Ernie. I'm happy to meet you. This is a truly grand old house here, isn't it?"

"Yes," Laura said, shaking his extended hand.

"Well, Ernest, the paperwork does look in order," Esther said. "Your name is really Ernest Gallo?"

"My parents had no imagination. Think how my brother Julio feels," he added with a chuckle. "You can call me Ernie. If it's all right with you two, I've got work to do," he said. "Help yourself to the coffee."

They watched as he walked back to the dining room, where he busied himself putting in a shim to level a window he had replaced.

Esther walked across the room and lifted the glass lid off of the crock pot. "Italian meatballs," she announced. "And, there's a baguette here, too."

The whistled notes of *Fly Me to the Moon* wafted through the rooms of the downstairs part of the house.

"At least we'll always know where he is," Esther said.

"NOW WHO'S THAT?" Esther asked. Someone was clomping up the front steps.

"Yoohoo! Anyone home? Oh my, do I smell lunch?"

Charmaigne, aspiring TV personality and designer extraordinaire, entered the house without knocking. Undaunted by the rain, she wore a strapless pink sundress, 4-inch heels and a charming bright yellow hardhat.

Her TV crew was following her, camera and lighting in hand.

She turned to the camera with a sweet smile.

"We here at the Street of Dreams are just one big happy family. We are in and out of each other's project houses all day."

"Hello ladies," she addressed Laura and Esther. *"Lorie* and *Ellen* are here working on the old Childers' house. Poor things. But someone had to draw this run-down place. Nice to see you again," she beamed as she air kissed first Laura and then Esther. Esther ducked dramatically but Laura returned the greeting with a forced smile.

"Lorie! Tell the people what your plans are for the house."

"It's actually Laura and . . ." Laura said before being interrupted again.

"Oh, I'm sure anything you do will be quaint and charming. When was this old place built? Do you know? Will you try to restore it or just give up and gut it? Did you just want to cry when you found out you were not decorating one of the new builds? Where is your builder, Russ? Is he on site today?"

"We here at Graham Construction were thrilled to..."

"OK," Charmaigne interrupted. "So nice to see both of you, and good luck on salvaging this place."

"CUT!" she yelled, as she pranced out the door and down the steps.

"Don't you just hate it when 'family' has to rush off like that and take their camera crew with them?' Esther asked.

She leaned out the door and yelled, "Break a leg."

"In this case, that's theater talk for "Break your damned leg!" she explained to Laura who was still standing with her mouth hanging open after the onslaught of Charmaigne and her crew.

"An empty room always looks smaller than a furnished one. It's the opposite with campsite tents."

10

Esther Graham noticed that Laura had put her laptop computer in the carrying case to take it to the building site. She assumed Laura was still researching the history of the Italianate building style. That's why she was surprised when Laura looked away from the computer screen later that morning to ask her a question.

"Did you know there were 603,106 people living in Portland last year?" Laura called over to Esther. "And there were 29 homicides during those 365 days," she added.

"No, but I know a lot of those still alive get to the McDonald's window at the same time I do every morning."

"That's one murder for every 20,707 people," Laura added.

"If you say so."

"So, why did Mr. Martinelli choose our place to die?" Laura asked.

"Laura, a murder victim, by definition, doesn't get to choose where they 'off' him."

"True," Laura said, "but I'm haunted by this. None of us knew the guy. No family members showed up at the funeral. Was he just walking around late at night waiting for his number to come up?"

"You'll drive yourself crazy if you can't put all this away in the back of your mind."

"I don't dwell on it on purpose," Laura said. "I want to know what happened to him so I can stop waiting for the next shoe to drop."

They heard Charmaigne clomping up the front porch steps again.

"You requested shoes? She's all yours," Esther said as she headed to the back of the house and left Laura to again welcome the flighty neighbor.

THE PORTLAND POLICE were back at the Dreams site when Laura and Esther arrived one morning. It was almost a month since Laura found Sal Martinelli's body and she was surprised to see the police moving from one home site to another, interviewing everyone on site.

Ernie was also there as promised and had brought cheese bagels for morning break.

Laura had a perfect perch and view out the upstairs landing window where she and Esther had been using spray bottles of fabric softener to loosen the old peach and green floral wallpaper they were stripping from the plaster walls.

Laura was surprised to see one of the officers carry a shovel to his car, open the trunk, and gently deposit the tool on a tarp. It looked like he and the detective were headed her way next. She moved downstairs to meet them at the door.

"Ms. Howard, may we come in?"

"It's so nice outside, why don't we use these porch benches?" she suggested. It was too early to start giving open house tours.

Detective Roberts and an officer she didn't recognize took a seat. Laura remained standing.

"We're talking to everyone on the project again," Detective Roberts said. "It's the Martinelli case," he added.

He thought she could have forgotten?

"We'd like to talk to you, Russell and Esther Graham."

"I can call Esther. She's upstairs, but Russ is out of town."

"For how long?"

"I don't really know," she said.

"You don't know when your business partner is returning?" the officer asked. "How soon did he start talking about leaving Portland after the cement incident in your driveway out here?"

"Maybe a week or two."

"And, you didn't find that strange?" he asked

"Not at all. He went back east to help with disaster relief after the New Jersey hurricane."

"And you haven't heard from him since?"

"No."

"How about Mrs. Graham?"

"Someone talking about me?" Esther asked as she stepped out onto the porch which was getting crowded.

The detective explained for the seventh time that day that he and the officer were still actively working on solving the Martinelli case and doing repeat interviews in the neighborhood. Esther surprised him by taking the offense.

"What have you found out so far?" she asked.

"We usually ask the questions."

"It seems like if you told us what you know already, it might jog something in our memories," Esther suggested. "You're back so you obviously think one of us was involved."

"Not at all," Detective Roberts said. "It may have been a burial of convenience not related to any of you. The man left a long list of victims in his wake."

"Sounds like we may be the only ones missing him," Esther said.

Laura rolled her eyes. She'd perfected the eye roll when she was a teenager and had never given it up completely. One could say so much with a good eye roll.

"From what we've found," Roberts said, "Sal Martinelli was heavy into gambling debt. He could have been snuffed to send a message to others."

"Martinelli's death would have gotten even more press coverage if Detective Roberts hadn't blocked the details of the incident," the officer said. "We won't be able to hold back info much longer."

"If he was losing money at Oregon casinos, wouldn't they have scalped him?" Esther asked.

Laura gasped. She knew there were times when Esther thrived on the shock value of a politically inappropriate statement, but this one was over the top.

Since the Indian Gaming Act in 1988, nine Indian casinos had been built in Oregon and a tenth was proposed. The federal act had met with a lot of controversy and litigation, but its overall purpose was pure. It provided a basis for the operation and regulation of Indian gaming and for the generation of revenue for the tribes. It encouraged economic development and also protected the casinos from negative influences (pronounced "mob activity.")

"Mrs. Graham," the detective said, "we weren't thinking of Oregon gambling. Martinelli had a pattern of flying in and out of Reno."

"Oh. So what's with the shovel?"

"You two don't miss much, do you?" Roberts asked. "We picked up the shovel because it had dried cement on it."

"Not unusual on a construction site. You think?" Laura asked.

Detective Roberts struggled to regain command of the interview.

"If you hear from Russell Graham, please notify us immediately. And, we'd prefer that you don't tell him that we were back today," he said. "In the meantime, please don't hesitate to call me directly if anything else occurs to you."

"Are you two alone here?" he asked as an afterthought.

"As a matter of fact, no."

"I hear whistling," he said.

"Fly Me to the Moon," the officer said, naming that tune in three notes.

"That's Ernie. He'll be working here until Russ gets back." Laura said.

"Did he work here before the murder?"

"No, Ernie's a new acquaintance," Esther said. "You're welcome to meet him, but I'd wait until the end of the chorus if I were you."

The two men returned to the police cruiser and rolled slowly down the street and back toward the downtown area.

"That was strange," Laura said.

"Maybe yes, maybe no," Esther answered.

"What do you know that you're not telling me?"

"I hadn't told you and I definitely wasn't telling them," Esther said. "A couple of strange entries came on the statement for Russ' business credit card. I wasn't going to mention them to you until I had a chance to call Mr. Visa."

"Strange how?"

"The charges are from places in Shreveport, Louisiana, instead of the East Coast."

"I thought the Louisiana hurricane was farther south than Shreveport."

"Farther south and several years ago," Esther said quietly.

"Do I have to pull this information from you bit by bit or do you just want to spill?"

"When I saw charges for The Naked Bean, I figured it was a coffee shop."

"OK."

"Not so much with a $465 charge at Alley Cats and another $630 at Chicky's Boom Boom Room on the same date," she said. "Those were both in Shreveport."

Laura looked stunned.

"There's also a hefty charge at Sin City Cabaret in New York. I checked that one out on the web and it's one of the top ten strip clubs in New York City."

"You're kidding me?"

"Wish I were."

"Russ?" Laura asked.

"There's got to be an explanation."

"Wanna bet?" Laura asked.

"Are you ladies OK in there?" Ernie called from the kitchen.

"Fine," they called back in unison.

"OH WHAT A TANGLED web we weave," Laura muttered. She'd been searching the Internet for over an hour and still hadn't found the inspiration she wanted for drapery fabric for the formal dining room. She didn't object to making drapes to save a little money. Most draperies only took four straight seams on two lengths of 56-inch material plus some decorative rings. But, she wanted a color palette that was snappy, not safe, and definitely didn't taunt "nya, nya, nya, nya neutral" at potential home buyers examining the room. The dining room needed to make a grand first impression.

It was easier to be creative before hand-stenciling went out of vogue. Give it a decade or two, and stenciling would be all the rage again. Decorating trends seemed to travel on a twenty-year time loop.

Browsing the Internet was worse than looking in old encyclopedias, she thought. You'd start out very driven and looking for one specific thing and then could easily spend an entire evening leaping from page to page or site to site.

She checked New Jersey news sites, scanning the hurricane damage photos again, looking closely to see if anyone had captured the work crews from Oregon in their films. Russ was an attractive guy, after all. You'd think someone would add a photo of one of the out-of-state volunteers for human interest, if not for the friends and family at home to verify his refreshing spirit of volunteerism—or his total deceit. All she saw, though, were news shots of unfortunate families and the occasional pet surveying the ruins with a family in a small boat. There wasn't even a mention of out-of-state volunteer teams working in the area. Maybe Russ hadn't intended to go there at all. Now, there was a new thought.

No. Russ wasn't like her late husband. But, history did repeat itself. As predictably as decorating fads.

She closed the computer, announced "lights out" to Louise, and went up to bed.

"Tomorrow's another day," she quoted to the cat. "That's it," she said. "We'll use scarlet for the drapes in that dining room."

"When making curtains, think 'three sheets to the wind(ow.)' The finished product should be two to three times the width of the glass."

11

The newly-washed dark blue pickup truck shone in the sunshine as Laura pulled into a parking place at Widmer's Hardware Store. The Big Box stores were OK for some items, but sometimes Laura wanted to talk with an employee who was familiar with the merchandise. She was looking for a brace she could ask Russ to pound in to steady the lattice work fencing around the gazebo behind the house when he returned. Not all of the original fencing could be saved, but she wanted to rescue as much as possible to add charm to the future landscaping.

Laura knew she had little to no landscaping skills. She liked the finished product when others made the plant choices and graded and contoured the soil in the yard for artistic affect, but she didn't know anything about operating rototillers or the depth to plant seedlings. She thought her best local source to help with the plant selection might be Jamen Childers. He had shown her the rough draft of landscaping plans for the house he and his mother were building and he seemed to know what he was doing. Besides, it would be nice to have the yards throughout the block compatible with one another.

She liked Jamen. He was a little on the soft side for her, but, Lord knew, he was a patient man. His role in life seemed to be to shepherd his mother about and mend fences behind her wherever she went. That woman was the exact opposite of her gentle son. Every time Francesca opened her mouth she offended one homebuilder or another on the block.

Laura thought if Francesca and Esther ever got into it, it'd be a tough call on where to place your bet.

"But the tickets would sell fast," she said aloud.

LAURA CLIMBED the stairs up to Esther's apartment the next morning. She found a hand-lettered sign on the front door: ELECTION PRECINCT NUMBER ONE

Laura knocked lightly, poked her head in, and called out, "Anyone home?"

"I'll be out in a minute," Esther answered.

She walked solemnly out of the bedroom with an addressed and stamped business-size envelope in her hand. She carefully placed the envelope in the woven wire basket she reserved for out-going mail.

"Did you remember it's Election Day?" Esther asked.

Oregon voters had been voting by mail for several years now, but Esther refused to give up the experience of going to the polls and casting a ballot. She always filled out her ballot while standing in her small walk-in closet using the low shelf as a desk.

Her civic duty completed, she crossed the room and removed the precinct sign. Laura elected not to comment.

"Lighten your entryway by replacing the wood panels in your front door with reed glass. It also makes your reflection look tall and thin."

12

Louise heard the back door at The Harrington close as Laura left for work He stretched his front paws, extending his claws to use the vintage runner on the hardwood floor as an exercise apparatus. Scratching posts were so passé.

Laura described the cat as "cute but incorrigible." Russ admired Louise's "attitude." Only Esther and Hammer understood that "a cat's gonna do what a cat's gonna do."

Louise flounced downstairs and leaped gracefully onto the small occasional table Laura had placed in front of the living room windows. The lace cloth slid off the table, taking the vintage lamp with it.

The cat was startled by the crashing sound, but recovered quickly and catapulted (bad pun!) himself back to the table top. He stretched out on the wood surface which had been warmed by the morning sun and began to bathe his soft orange fur. Louise' job description was not lengthy. Sleep, play, eat.

LAURA OFTEN FELT scattered. There were so many design projects at the Italianate home that she knew couldn't be completed until Russ returned. She had tentatively chosen colors and fabrics for the living room, but couldn't tell for sure until she knew how much light would fill the room. And, she wouldn't know that until she knew if Russ planned to put glass-paneled doors or sliding panels in to make it possible for the new owners to separate the living room from the dining room.

Was he planning on shadowed glass or stained glass for the bathroom windows? Were the closet doors to be shuttered or paneled?

She had been up and downstairs twice this Monday morning, trying to list the remaining work in her head. She planned to tackle the grand entry next, but she was hesitant. She wanted to use Venetian burnished plaster for the walls in that space to give them a warm, luminescent look when folks first entered. There was a major problem, though: She had only read about Venetian plaster finishes, never applied one. She was sitting on the second stair of the grand staircase with her head in her hands, when she heard Ernie coming her way. He was light of foot, but consistently announced his whereabouts by his whistled musical selections. Was that *Stardust* he was whistling?

"You look troubled," he said.

"I'm a little at odds," Laura said. "What do you know about applying Venetian plaster?"

"Not bragging, mind you, but I know just about everything there is to know about it. Used to do a lot of that finish work before I started specializing in laying tile. . . ."

Laura looked relieved.

"Just saying," Ernie added.

Laura had seen shots of Ernie's tile work stored on his cell phone, and the man was an artist. He brushed off any compliments, but his work was brilliant.

"I don't even know whether I'm supposed to tackle the job before or after you do the tile work in the entry," she said.

"Have you ever spread plaster?" he asked.

Laura shook her head.

"Then, definitely, before I lay the tile. It'll give you more freedom to drop some while you're learning. That is, if you'll let me teach you."

Laura drove out to the nearest building supply store. She ordered the plaster mixed with marble dust in a warm butter cream tone. The store clerk insisted on picking out a trowel for her, explaining to her that she'd need one with rounded corners so a novice plasterer wouldn't leave scratches and lines on the wall. She didn't mention that she would be said plasterer or that the tool looked to her like it could be used to flip pancakes when she was through with this job.

Ernie and Esther were waiting for her when she returned to the job site. He had finished replacing the chair rail in the library and Esther had tired of bookkeeping tasks at Graham Construction and come by to check on the progress at the Dreams place.

Laura had seen interior plastering done many times in the past. She wasn't sure, though, what caused Venetian plaster to have the depth of color and slight sheen when the job was finished.

"It goes on in several layers," Ernie explained. "Pretend you're a very stingy baker and you're icing a cake. Hold the trowel at a 45-degree angle, scraping the plaster onto the wall. Use large sweeping motions," he said as he demonstrated. "After the first coat, there may be some of the cake—or wall in this case—showing through. That's OK."

Ernie supervised while she put on the first coat, then called for a lunch break. After that coat dried, he said they'd apply a slightly thicker layer of plaster that would cover the exposed areas she missed with the first coat.

"I expected this to shine more, look more like stone," Laura said.

"It will," Ernie assured her. "We'll sand down the later layers. Then we'll wipe down the walls with damp rags. I like to apply three coats when we're dealing with an entryway," he said. "Then comes the sanding.

Here's the secret," he said in a confidential tone. "The smoother the finish is, the shinier the luster will be."

Laura was in awe. She felt like Ernie had trusted her enough to share his family recipe for meatballs.

Four days later the entryway walls shone like glass. Except for the splotches on the subflooring where the plaster had gotten away from Laura, the job was beautiful. And, Ernie, master of tile and whistled medleys, would cover those marks when he set the tile.

Esther had heard so much about the plaster job as it progressed, that she brought Hammer to the site with her so they could both see the result.

She admired the warm glow of the room. Finally she asked Laura if Ernie was there.

"Listen," Laura said. "That's how I always find him. It'll usually be either *Stars Fell on Alabama* or *Fly Me to the Moon.*"

"Sounds like he's got an astronomy theme going," Esther observed. She walked to the back part of the house to see him.

WHEN LAURA TRIED to roll out of bed the next morning, her back and shoulders ached in places she didn't know she had muscles to strain. Ernie's advice to make "wide swoops" when applying plaster the last few days had apparently taken a toll on her.

She had also panicked and clipped her left shin on the table leg when she returned to The Harrington late the night before. She had unlocked the back door, pressed in the numbers on the control panel of the alarm system Russ had insisted that she have installed, and then moved into the dining room.

She saw the shattered lamp on the floor and immediately assumed burglars had beaten her home. As she was rubbing her wounded leg, she recalled that the alarm system would have blasted if that were the case. A quick survey told her all of the downstairs windows were locked and both exit doors were also locked when she arrived.

As she stood there trying to relax after her initial fright, Louise scampered down the stairs and demanded his dinner.

"Aha!" she said.

The cat wasn't talking. He brushed his soft fur against her leg and then struck a pose that was supposed to make Laura feel guilty for leaving him alone all day. It worked. She picked him up and carried him to the kitchen to see what she could serve for their evening meals.

Laura knew that Louise probably expected a quiet candlelit four-course dinner, but he'd have to settle for a can of cat food. That antique lamp had been expensive.

"Vintage charm has its limits. For every leaded glass window, there's a leak."

13

The police cruiser drove past slowly and Laura exhaled. She had been scraping wallpaper from the parlor for several hours and was covered in dried bits of paper and what had become papier-mâché when the warm water combined with the dried wallpaper paste. She had an entire wall left to attack and wasn't in the mood to answer any more questions from the police.

Had it been modern wallpaper she might have cheated and painted right over it. The paper was so old, though, that it had been hung with a half-inch overlap between sheets. She could see the faded words printed vertically along the overlap. The maker wanted the paperhanger to be aware that there was a 12-inch drop in the pattern.

Laura dropped to the floor with her back against the wall to rest. She had packed a cooler with a cheese and tomato sandwich, an apple and a couple cans of Coke.

"The real thing. All the calories, all the color, all the caffeine," she said.

She turned to see police Detective Chris Pfeifer standing in the doorway. She hadn't seen him since he helped solve the mystery surrounding her husband's death.

"Well, just walk right in, why don't you?"

"Laura, the front door is off the hinges," he said.

"I've got it out back on sawhorses so I can sand it this afternoon."

"So, you're not taking the recent threats as seriously as the department suggested?" he asked.

"Guilty as charged." She struggled to her feet. "I would have heard someone come in."

"Yeah. Like you heard me."

"Point taken," she said. "It's nice to see you. It's been awhile."

She respected Pfeifer's opinion. He had solved the mystery around her husband's death. And she owed him for saving her life too. She just didn't like to be told what to do. And, there were deadlines to meet on remodeling this house, she told him. It was hard enough to line up subcontractors without having to reschedule them because her part of the work wasn't completed. In this case she wanted the walls stripped before the electrician arrived to install period wall sconces.

"Is this a social call?" she asked.

She'd forgotten how good looking the guy was. Pfeifer stood 5 foot 10, but his manner made him seem much taller. He looked like he worked out regularly but was lean, not muscle bound. She remembered his thick long eyelashes from the first time they'd met. She'd die for those—and she might have died if Pfeifer hadn't been there to protect her two years ago.

"This stop is purely professional. The guys working the case think you might be more willing to talk to me," he said. "They're not having any luck finding Russ."

"And I might have him hidden in the pantry here?"

"Has he called in?"

"No."

"Not in two weeks?" he asked. "He has a cell phone, right?"

"Look. I'd tell you if I knew what's going on with him," she said. "I thought your guys could trace cell phones."

"We suspect he doctored the phone so it can't be located by the police."

"That works?

"Without cell tower triangulation, a cell phone's just a piece of plastic."

Late last night Laura had been thinking strangulation, not triangulation, where Russ was concerned.

"Would Russ know that? The man didn't learn to text until last month."

"He'd know that," Pfeifer said simply. "If you hear from him or if he resurfaces here, could you ask him to call me immediately?"

"If Mr. Graham and I are speaking by then, I'll do that."

Pfeifer didn't envy Russell Graham when the man did return to Portland.

"In the meantime," he said, "can I have a tour of this project?"

She tossed him the other can of Coke which exploded over his hand when he yanked the pull tab.

"I probably had that coming," he said. "I told Roberts you wouldn't be holding back information."

She showed Pfeifer through the downstairs rooms and then they made their way carefully up the staircase. The stairs were in good repair for the age of the house, but not yet illuminated well enough to meet current building code standards. Another job for an electrician. Russ knew his limitations and always subcontracted the wiring and plumbing.

If Russ didn't return soon, the old house might be the first uncompleted nightmare on the Street of Dreams.

She gave Pfeifer the 50-cent tour of the house before he headed back to work. Laura got into her truck, pulled out right behind him, and drove toward The Harrington. Ernie could board up the front entrance before he left for the day.

THE MULTIPLE FIREPLACES in the Dreams' house were one of the things that appealed most to Laura about the late nineteenth-century style of architecture. True, she and Russ had hired an air conditioning/heating contractor to bring the climate control up to date—and so the old house would meet current standards. But Laura found the fireplaces charming all the same.

She and Russ had agreed to restore the fireplaces in the living room, parlor, and master bedroom so they could be used by the future owners. Laura would draw attention to the other two fireplaces as focal points in the rooms by adding decorative ornate screens and light sconces. She planned to add framed art pieces to set on the ornate mantels and balance against the plastered walls. She wasn't going to be the first to drive a nail through that newly painted wall.

"Self-priming paint isn't! It will take more research and development before this product cuts the mustard—or any other bright color."

14

The large expanse of old hardwood floor inside the Dreams house looked as if it had been turned into a giant Scrabble board. Ernie had brought colored tile samples with him this morning and he and Laura were trying to decide on a pattern for the flooring tiles that would be placed in the entryway.

She was leaning toward a rust-colored tile with lighter shades veining through it.

"I'm a little leery of that one," Ernie advised. "It could be awfully slick in an entryway in a rainy climate."

He reached across the mock Scrabble board to where he had some boxes of smaller tiles.

"What would happen if we put these lighter colored pieces between some of the rust ones? Would that give you the same intensity of color you want?" he asked.

"Wouldn't that take more time and be more expensive?"

"Both," Ernie said. "But these little babies have a textured top and, if we placed them just right, they could prevent people in wet shoes from taking a spill. The ones you're considering are pretty, but the choice might come back to bite us."

Laura started moving tiles around again, but was uncertain.

"Let's get smart here," Ernie said. "Let's play this game on the entryway floor so you can see how it would look in the actual light where the tile floor will be."

"I wish I'd said that," Laura said.

They laid out the entryway floor in the warm rust tiles Laura had selected. The light bounced off the tile nicely when the front door was open, but the room appeared much too dark at other times.

"Time to regroup," Laura said. "Let's try some of the lighter colored textured tiles for the main floor and use the rust ones for accents. Less slippery and a better blend with the wall colors."

One practice layout later and they had the ideal pattern.

"I'll be right back," Ernie said. "Don't touch those."

He came back in the room with his cell phone and took photographs of the pattern.

"Smart man, Ernie," Laura said.

He waltzed out of the room to the ending notes of *Fly Me to the Moon.*

LAURA HEARD SOMEONE coming in the front door and she headed that way. Before she could stop him, Ward Simmons had stepped inside the Dreams house.

"You here all alone?" he asked. "Where's Esther's boyfriend Ernie?"

"Two steps behind you and ready to strike," Ernie said from the front porch. "Did I just see you walk into this lady's house without even so much as a knock or a shout out?"

"That's my right. It's in my job description," Simmons said.

"Not in this house. Out!" Ernie commanded in a loud voice that made Laura question whether she too should leave.

Ward took a half step back and looked Ernie up and down. Ernie was a short, stocky man, and he looked able to take care of himself. He was getting ready to lay the tile in the entryway and he was wearing knee pads over his Levis.

"You takin' up skate boarding?" Ward asked.

Ernie slowly reached to retrieve a trowel he had jammed uncomfortably in his back pants pocket.

"Don't shoot! Don't shoot!" Ward yelled.

"You're dumber than you are obnoxious," Ernie said. "It's a trowel. How many building sites have you been on in your short life?"

"Now, look here," Ward said.

"I don't want to look. And I don't want to see you here again. Next time it might just be a gun."

Ernie waved the hand trowel menacingly and Ward left. They heard Simmons mumbling something about "seeing about that," a citizen's rights, and knowing people in high places.

IT WAS LATE afternoon when Detective Christopher Pfeifer arrived. Laura missed the days when he was Officer Chris Pfeifer and wore the standard-issue uniform of the Portland Police Bureau. He still had the little boy look and the rosy cheeks from when Laura first met him, but he looked a tad less dashing in a sports coat. He hadn't lost the easy, relaxed manner and the wide grin, though. And, he knocked and waited on the front porch of the Dreams house until he was asked inside.

"Have you had trouble out here today?" he asked.

"Here?" Laura repeated. "No more than usual," she said.

"In your case, that doesn't tell me much," he said, his face relaxing in that ready smile.

"I don't *cause* the trouble," she said defensively.

"Agreed. It seems to follow you, though, wherever you go."

He stepped inside and slipped out of his coat. The downstairs of the house was cooler than the upstairs rooms, but it still held the heat from one summer day to the next.

Chris Pfeifer had admired Laura Howard when they worked together to solve her husband's murder. He'd been quite attracted, but that certainly wasn't the time to ask her out. Now that he'd run into her again, the answer was still "no." She was a witness—at the very least—in this current case.

"We got a call from a citizen named Edward Simmons. He said there was someone on your work site carrying a concealed weapon without a permit."

Laura turned and called out to the kitchen where Ernie was taking a late afternoon break. "Hey, Ernie, have you got a minute? There's someone here I'd like you to meet."

Ernie came in, chomping on the remains of an apple.

"Excuse my manners," he said. "Just finishing up my break." He reached for his back pocket to get a handkerchief to wipe the apple juice from his hands.

"Not so fast," Pfeifer said. "Keep your hands where I can see them."

Ernie looked surprised—and a little hurt—but complied.

"Are you Ernest Gallo?" Pfeifer asked.

Ernie nodded and Pfeifer turned to Laura.

"Ernest Gallo? That's his real name?"

"He says his parents were imagination-impaired," she said. "His little brother is Julio."

"Like I'd buy that one."

"Ernie isn't armed. Unless you count a trowel and some blue-chalked string," she added. "Why don't you tell him what this is about?"

Pfeifer explained the reason for his trip to the site was to verify the information in a caller's report.

"That twit," was all Ernie could say as he stood there, shaking his head. "Please search me so I can get back to work. Laura can tell you all about Edward Simmons."

LAURA STOOD in the front yard where she could better examine the outside of the Dreams house. She knew Russ would hire professional painters to take care of the exterior painting, but she wanted to be certain the front entry porch would entice house hunters. She decided to tackle painting that area herself.

She had dressed for the job at hand. She said a silent prayer that Joan Rivers, Kelly Osborn and TV's Fashion Police squadron wouldn't be filming in the area.

She had selected her wardrobe pieces carefully that morning. Faded black sweat bottoms, a tight tank top to keep paint scraping debris from sliding down her neckline, and Russ' paint-stained flannel shirt he hadn't taken with him. She added work boots that were a size too large (but who could pass up a good sale price?)

The front porch needed to have the authentic vintage look to add to buyers' first impression of the place and

Ripped, Stripped and Flipped

to accent the blend of Italianate features and modern décor she planned to use in the interior.

Inside she'd use high gloss white enamel on the window surrounds for a fresh, sanitized look. "Vintage" was great, but no one wanted to worry that those were lead paint chips instead of parmesan bread crumbs floating in their soup.

She let her mind wander. A cold soup and salad "combo" would be good to order on a day like this. She hadn't been out to a nice restaurant recently. Not since Russ left. Russ and his credit card who seemed to be dining in high style nightly . . .

She could go out if she really wanted to, she thought. She was still smarting from Russ suggesting that she do just that while he was gone. Laura hadn't only imagined that they were a couple. Russ had made it very clear to her two or three weeks before his exit that he wanted to take the relationship to the next level.

When he's here, he introduces me to his friends as his girlfriend, she remembered. He calls me most nights before bed. He buys me flowers and can't seem to stop touching me when we talk, a pat here, a soft touch there. So what's the urgency of this particular hurricane? As far as I know, he didn't take off for Katrina.

Russ and Laura had known each other for four years. In the beginning they were employer and employee. It progressed to employer/protector and employee. Next was friend and business partner.

Laura knew she had major trust issues after her marriage to Todd Howard. But she was past all that and no longer mourned his loss or missed the "good times" once she realized even the good times with Todd were all a sham. Todd had been a liar, a crook, a thief and a cheater—and those were her kind words.

Maybe she had too vehemently declared she would never marry again when she first met Russ. OK. So she had been a tad bitter, but she was ready to move on now.

She and Russ had shared countless work lunches in the past two years, several romantic dinners out and day trips to the coast. They had discussed children and religious beliefs. Russ had declared he didn't believe in live-in arrangements before marriage. He claimed it took the mystery out of a relationship and belittled the commitment of the marriage ceremony.

Laura had to admit to herself that she was in love with the guy. If Russ wanted mystery in their relationship, he was certainly providing it now. Hadn't he heard of Sprint or Cellular One? Why no contact?

"Go to sleep," she told herself. She glanced at the clock and groaned. It was 2 a.m. and she was lying here trying to figure out Russell Graham.

She remembered him holding her hand and escorting her upstairs to the bedroom at The Harrington. Apparently that night together was the highest level he could commit to before he took off for disaster rcstoration.   She kicked herself for being so gullible. She'd thought Russ was the real thing.

Maybe *she* needed a night out. Nothing fancy, but a chance to see other people her own age.

"Well-polished hardwood floors remain a delightful way to showcase your dust bunnies."

15

After a shower and shampoo, Laura felt like a new woman. She chose a spaghetti strap dress that had hung unworn in her closet for two summers. She had intended to let down the hem when she found the dress on a sale rack. Instead, she put on flat sandals tonight and the hem automatically dropped two inches. Instant alterations.

A manicure and pedicure were long overdue and she tended to those next.

This was the start of her effort to move back into the Portland social world. She would have preferred to be staying home with Louise, watching a movie and munching on microwave popcorn, but she suspected now that Russ had been serious when he'd suggested that she go out while he was gone.

She parked the truck on the well-lit side of a new "dinner place" (Esther's description) and did her best imitation of confident diner as she entered. She passed the "please seat yourself sign," and headed toward a small booth near the side entrance. A tall man stepped sideways and blocked her path.

"Could I buy you a drink? Maybe something red and yellow?"

"Officer Orange?" Laura asked, not sure she recognized the cop out of uniform.

He held out his arms and gave her a big hug. He was definitely better in street clothes doing the bar scene than he had been hanging in the driver's side window of her truck, waving a warning notice. Chinos, a long-sleeved muted striped shirt. And, were those Tevas?

"Pete Swensen," he said introducing himself. "And, you would be Miss Hostility?"

"Laura," she reminded him. It was the first time she'd been to this place and she'd had no idea it was a cop hangout.

He ordered a margarita for her and another beer for himself. He helped her through the mob scene and selected a small booth off to the side. She sensed this wasn't his first beer, but figured he was off duty and that was his business.

He eased into the booth on the same side of the table where she was sitting. She hated it when guys did that without being invited. He toyed with the candle on the table for a minute, then caught her off guard when he asked if she'd heard anything more about "your body."

She looked puzzled.

"The hand? You do remember the hand you found?" he asked.

"Of course. I try not to think about it." She was also trying not to think about his hand that had just landed on her bare knee under the table.

"Good plan. What do you think about dancing?"

He stumbled a little getting up and out of the booth, but guided her smoothly out to the dance floor, a tight square of wood parquet set in a herringbone pattern. She'd questioned his alcohol intake earlier, and now she suspected he wouldn't have to lead on the dance floor. She could just follow the fumes. As she was deciding it would be a one-dance limit, his hand traveled down her back and cupped her butt. She moved his hand back where it belonged, but it travelled north, up under her arm and began groping.

"That's it," she said pulling back. She stepped back and was about to deliver a sharp elbow to his ribs when she heard a familiar voice.

"Hey, Laura," Detective Pfeifer said.

"Hey, yourself," she answered a bit too loudly as she spotted him moving toward her and her dance partner. He cut in and moved her toward the other side of the tiny dance floor, then danced her out the exit to an outdoor patio covered with painted trellis and small white lights.

"Thanks," she said, "but I was about to take care of that situation in there."

"I know you were," Pfeifer said, "but Swensen doesn't have any sick leave left. I thought I should rescue you both."

"You know that guy?" she asked.

"He was my former partner in the bureau. That's one of the reasons I was eager to make detective," he said. "The question is how do you know him?"

"He pulled me over last month. He seemed nice enough, saw me home safely. . ."

"Crap. I suppose he told you it was a welfare check."

"How did you know that?" she asked.

"And, then he worked his way into your house?"

Laura nodded.

"Did I teach you nothing the last time we worked together?" he asked.

"I know he's drunk tonight, but is he that bad?"

"Pete's an OK guy when he's not drinking. A little crass is all."

"Define 'a little crass,'" she said.

"Well, I'd never introduce him to my sisters."

"Now there's a test," she said.

Pfeifer offered to take her home, but she opted to have him walk her safely across the dark parking lot to the truck instead. She'd only had two sips of the margarita. She knew she was safe to drive. She also knew that Pfeifer would probably make sure that Pete Swensen didn't get behind the wheel.

She had been interested in dating Pfeif once, but it never came about. Maybe someday.

"Fresh semi-gloss paint on crown molding and baseboards gives a room the well-groomed look of a new mani and pedi."

16

Laura had driven around to the back entry of the project house to a barren spot where the lawn had once been. The oversized lot would make a great backyard for kids someday. This morning it was a mud flat.

She could hear Ernie already at work as she stood in the drizzle digging in her purse for her house key. *Stars Fell on Alabama*. He was really quite good.

As she stepped onto the porch to place her key in the back door, she glanced to her right. What had looked like a stack of used painters' drop cloths when she approached the porch now looked more ominous. There was a woman's boot sticking out of the rolled up cloths.

Laura screamed when she saw blood on the light colored suede boot. She shrieked again when the boot didn't move after her first loud greeting.

Ernie met her on the other side of the back door. He opened the door and she rushed in, dialing her cell phone as she went. She hit the numbers on the phone precisely, leaving no room for error. She had memorized the number for Roberts' private line when he had given it to her earlier.

"Detective Roberts.

She heard the gruff voice through the background noise at the police bureau.

"I've got another one."

"One what?" asked Detective Roberts. "Illegal parker, graffiti artist?"

"No. No. Of course not. A ..."

"Ms. Howard, you're going to have to work with me here. Two syllables? Starts with?" he asked, trying to help her.

"A body."

"Of course you do. That's why you had to beat off Swensen at the bar," he said calmly.

Obviously, the story had spread.

"No. A *dead* body!"

"Are you sure?" he asked.

"There's blood and it didn't move when I screamed at it."

"Is it someone you know?"

"I don't think so."

"And, it sounds like it may be too late for introductions," he said. "Again."

She looked out the window

"Oh S-H-I-T. It moved."

"Call 911. That's what you should have done in the first place," he said. He let the other detective in the office know that he would be out for a while. He reached for his coat, signaled Anderson to join him, and they raced for the parking lot where their car was waiting.

WHOEVER WAS UNDER the fabric groaned. Laura moved forward cautiously.

The crumpled body tucked into the alcove on the back porch was wearing Charmaigne's mauve sweater. Laura glanced at the feet and now recognized the expensive boots with silver fur and sequins festooned around the tops. These from the woman who last week was wearing wedge sandals with perfect toe cleavage showing . . .

"Where am I?" Charmaigne asked.

Laura didn't tell her that was an overused line from TV soap operas. This was no time to be judgmental.

"Don't move," she said. "I've called 911 and I hear sirens."

"But, my hair. . ."

Laura looked at the blood matting Charmaigne's hair to the woman's scalp, and she felt sick. "It never looked better," she said. "Try not to worry about that. Are you warm enough?"

Before Charmaigne could answer, a red and white rescue unit pulled up at the house and uniformed men carrying boxes filled with equipment joined them on the porch. The EMT's covered Charmaigne with a foil lined blanket and began taking vital signs, quickly relaying the information by phone to emergency personnel at the hospital. Ten minutes later, Charmaigne was lifted onto a stretcher and transported to Emanuel Medical Center. "For further evaluation," the medics said.

Laura was left standing on the blood-stained porch. She should be doing something, but she wasn't sure what. She was still a little shook by her latest call for the police. She asked Ernie to jog across the lots and contact Gary Young, the builder with whom Charmaigne had been working for the past several months. Surely he'd know someone to contact in case of an emergency.

Gary Young was soft spoken, calm, and all-business on the project—a modified craftsman two-story house— where he and Charmaigne had been working. In fact, his stature, gait and work style reminded Laura a lot of Russ.

Russ, who apparently didn't care enough to call Oregon to see how his own project was going . . . How could she miss him so much and be mad at him at the same time, she wondered.

PORTLAND'S FINEST were back. They were the last people Laura wanted to see. She was still mortified by having made another bumbled phone call to the police.

She handled business calls in a perfectly calm, efficient, and professional manner, Laura had explained to Esther yesterday. But, when it came to reporting bodies to the police, she went all flibbertyjibbit.

"I should hope so," Esther had said. "I think the cops would be suspicious if you chatted about the weather for a while and then added 'by the way, there's a corpse out here with me.'"

Today the police were back to ask questions about Charmaigne.

"The vague description the victim provided of her assailant could fit any number of construction workers," Detective Roberts said. "She remembers a plaid shirt, Levis, a tool belt and a yellow hardhat."

"That could be anyone," Laura said.

"Has your missing partner Graham returned?"

"I can't believe you asked me that," Laura answered.

"You know the story. Everyone's a suspect," he said. "And Russell Graham fits the description, right down to the flannel shirt, vest and hard hat."

"It's a construction site!" Laura exploded.

"I have to ask these questions, ma'am," he said.

It was hard not to respond to the latest "mamming," but Laura contained herself.

"Do you know how many people within 1,000 feet of the house Charmaigne was decorating have probably thought they'd like to smack her?" Laura asked.

"Including you?"

"Absolutely," Laura said without hesitation. "Daily."

"For curiosity, where would you start if you were looking for a suspect out here in Dream Land?"

"Street of Dreams," she corrected him. "And, I'd start by interviewing anyone who had to spend more than ten minutes a day in the woman's vicinity."

"That bad?"

"That bad," she said.

"Blood stains can be removed from porous surfaces with a poultice of water, powdered detergent and chlorine bleach, or covered discreetly with a tasteful pot of bright red and white variegated geraniums."

17

Fletcher was particularly active this morning. The bird's drilling was accompanied by a shrill *ki, ki ki ki* call which was driving Laura nuts. She'd checked the Internet and learned that northern flickers primarily nested in trees, making a three-inch opening and lining the nest with wood chips. Fine. But, this one sounded like he'd taken up residence in the walk-in closet in her bedroom.

The web site was a world of information, telling her that the birds were ground feeders, eating ants with occasional fruits, berries and seeds as optional menu choices. It repeated what Russ had told her about the birds drumming on metal or wood to declare their territory, noting that one northern flicker in Wyoming could be heard drumming on an abandoned tractor from a half-mile away.

"Lord, help us," she muttered under her breath. Maybe she could arrange a flight plan for Fletch to visit relatives in Wyoming over the holidays.

Laura, on the other hand, knew that *she* needed to visit Charmaigne and she couldn't wait until the holidays to do it.

CHARMAIGNE WAS in the hospital for her injuries and, Laura suspected, to get some nourishment through her veins. The injuries were not life threatening, but she'd be nursing a couple of broken ribs and multiple bruises for some time. Despite her head wounds and the stitched gash above her eyebrow, she was coherent and talking. And talking. And talking.

Esther, who had retired after a nursing career divided among three hospital emergency rooms in the Seattle area, assured Laura that no ER doctor would fail to notice the malnourished condition of a patient who arrived for help. In Charmaigne's case, the injuries that sent her to the ER could save her life. She had told the police and the doctors about the beating she had suffered.

Laura's hope was that the injuries would lead to a prolonged in-house rehabilitation program. A program long enough that the Dreams homes could be finished before the woman was released. Between Fletch at home and Charmaigne at work, there had been constant chatter for the past several months.

Laura didn't wish the woman ill. But, that was what hospitals were for, wasn't it?

THAT AFTERNOON LAURA stopped by the hospital to pay a brief call on Charmaigne. If Esther could stand to visit the woman for over an hour, Laura figured she could last 20 minutes.

Detective Roberts and an officer arrived at the door to the hospital room right behind Laura. Roberts told Charmaigne they needed her help to answer a few questions.

"Do you know Russell Graham, Ma'am?" the detective asked.

"That rhymes," Charmaigne said. "Do you get it? You're so clever."

"Yeah, that's him," the officer said with a smirk.

Charmaigne's bottom lip was stitched, but she tried her best to smile at the detective and his partner. The detective shot the younger man a warning look and turned back to Charmaigne.

"Did you know Graham before this project started?"

"No. But, I wish I had," she said. "We were just getting acquainted when he kind of disappeared."

"Disappeared?"

"Well, the story is that he went back East to help hurricane victims, and that would be so like him. He's such a sweet man. But . . ."

"You don't think that's true?"

"I just find it hard to believe is all. Last time I saw him we were joking about gathering all the builders together and taking off for a project in a dry climate," she said. "We were just getting acquainted and, well, I just knew Russell and I were going to be better friends." She hesitated, then added, "If you know what I mean."

"What do you mean?"

"It felt like we had a connection. I'm working with a contractor who doesn't appreciate talent and Mr. G. . ."

"Mr. G.?"

"That's my little pet name for Russell. Anyway, my contractor doesn't realize that I'm the best designer in the area, and Russ is working with a woman who isn't formally certified as a designer."

"And?"

"It wouldn't be the first job site where a little swappin' went on. Again, if you know what I mean."

Laura took two steps forward before the officer stepped in front of her.

"Let me at her," she said under her breath. "Let me get in one good swing."

"Ms. Howard. That's not like you."

"It would have been if you hadn't stopped me," she told him. "Are you going to listen to this tripe?"

"We take down all information," he said. "But we evaluate its validity later at the station."

"The woman is delusional," Laura said.

"Officer? Is that a good thing or a bad thing she just said about me?"

"In summer, place a tall potted palm in front of a tri-fold room divider. After two or three glasses of wine, you'll think you've moved to The Bahamas."

18

The day after Laura visited Charmaigne in the hospital, Esther and Laura were going off site for lunch. They were both ready for something other than a sack lunch or Italian meatballs, but wouldn't have hurt Ernie's feelings by saying so. Laura insisted that Esther select the place and Esther chose the French restaurant across town.

"And, I'm not settling for the soup and salad special this time," Esther said. "I'm having the sausage-and-something-filled-parmesan-spinach pasta with soup, salad, an extra order of breadsticks and dessert. Maybe two desserts."

They were waiting for their entree when Laura said "There's something way wrong here."

"Maybe it's the salad dressing. We can ask the cook to check the pull date on the container," Esther answered.

"Nothing's wrong with the salad. But, something's definitely wrong with Russ. I was thinking about not hearing anything from him in over two weeks. What's wrong with the guy?"

"You think he's been hurt?" Esther asked.

"No. I think he's not behaving like a normal human being. He's not even behaving like a normal human being of the male gender," Laura added.

"Say how."

"Let's try for an almost believable scenario here," Laura said. "For instance, say he lost his phone and was stung by mega mosquitos. He got typhoid fever from the infested waters, plus he has somehow lost his voice and has both hands bandaged from the fingers clear up above the elbows . . ."

"*This* is your almost believable scenario?"

"Work with me here, Esther," Laura pleaded. "Let's assume the guy can't phone and he can't write."

"OK."

"But, don't you think with all the volunteers back there that he could have someone contact me? Or, couldn't Russ catch a ride into the nearest town that's not under water and send a telegram?"

"Possibly," Esther said. "He told us both he needed some time to sort things out."

"I thought he meant an hour or two in front of a televised football game," Laura said.

"I don't know what's going on with him, but he's obviously struggling with some sort of decision. I say we give him some time."

"I say three weeks is two weeks past the time limit," Laura said. "I'm all for the strong, silent type, but this feels like desertion."

"Maybe he only has use of one finger on his left hand and eventually he'll figure out he can send one of those text messages you guys use?" Esther suggested.

"I'd settle for something like 'wish you were here. Or, be back FTASB," Laura said.

"You want him to call you at fat-assed b-tch?"

"FTASB is text code for 'faster than a speeding bullet,'" Laura explained.

"Oh."

"I don't need a three page letter. I'd settle for BS," Laura confided.

"Some man sending me BS wouldn't light my fire," Esther said. "Not even in the old days when I had kindling to light."

"'BS' is text for 'big smile.'"

"Wait a minute. I may be in trouble here," Esther said. "Do you remember that e-mail message you sent me about lunch out today?"

"Yes."

"Tell me that LOL meant 'Lunch On Laura.'"

LAURA HAD A LONG history of hating telemarketers.

It was early evening and she and Louise had just settled down on the couch in the living room at The Harrington when the phone rang again. She'd already disengaged politely from a fund-raising call from University of Oregon and hung up on sales pitches from two insurance companies and Life Alert. The last one she found particularly offensive because the message was aimed toward senior citizens. Admittedly, she'd probably aged some from the fright of finding Mr. Martinelli, but nearing 30 years old didn't qualify her for senior discounts at Arby's yet.

The phone rang again. Maybe she could count the trips across the room to pick up the receiver as an exercise plan. Her cell phone was reserved only for business calls.

"This is the operator. Will you accept a collect call from Russell Graham?"

"Probably," she said.

"I need a 'yes' or 'no' answer."

"Can you stall a minute so he thinks I'm still debating?" Laura asked.

"The party can hear all your responses, Ma'am."

"Oh. Then, I'm dreadfully busy now, but he might try again in an hour," Laura said and hung up.

She went upstairs to wash and dry her clean hair. She was coming down again when the phone rang. A different operator's voice repeated the same message.

"If I must," Laura said.

"I'll take that as a 'yes,'" the operator responded and Russ' voice came on the line.

"What the hell is the problem?"

"Those of us who stayed in Portland don't have any problems. Unless, of course, we count covering your backside with the police and not sharing any information about your adult entertainment habits . . ."

"What?" he asked.

"Was there something you wanted when you placed this call?"

"Originally, I wanted to tell you how much I've missed you," he said. "Now, I'm not so sure."

"Then, I'm hanging up."

"Wait," he said. "I'm flying into PDX on United Thursday at 5:10 p.m."

Laura didn't respond.

"Can you pick me up?" he asked quietly.

"Yes."

"Good. I'll see you then," he said, but she had already hung up.

TRAFFIC WAS HEAVIER than she'd anticipated and when she arrived at PDX, Laura parked the truck on the third level of short-term parking and sprinted across the enclosed skywalk to the terminal. She looked at a monitor and found that a United flight from EWR was due in at 5:10 p.m. If she ran, she could make it to the area where he would be waiting for his baggage. She had to remember to ask him why an airport in Trenton, New Jersey, was abbreviated EWR. The topic might come up on *Jeopardy* someday.

When she got there, Russ was standing by his duffel bag, shifting from foot to foot on the wildly printed commercial carpet which Laura guessed had been chosen by a committee.

"A good flight?" she asked.

"When I didn't see you here, I thought you'd changed your mind about picking me up."

"No," she said. "I misjudged traffic. I know better. I should have predicted what things would be like between 4 and 6 p.m." She hesitated and then added, "The truck's in short term parking."

"Laura," he said. "What's going on? No hug 'hello?'"

"Sure," she said and gave him a brief one-armed hug.

"Let's get to the house," she said. "Then, we have some serious talking to do."

"Looks like," he said. "You won't believe all the crap that happened to me back East."

"Probably not."

ESTHER WAS WAITING for them at Graham Construction and invited them up to her place for a meal. Laura tried to beg off, but not even she was that strong when Esther mentioned the lemon meringue pie she'd whipped up for dessert. Laura was infuriated with Russ, but she hadn't gone stupid overnight. Besides, it might help to have Esther there as a referee.

As they sat down to eat, Laura heard a cell phone ringing. She looked expectantly at Russ, waiting for him to answer it.

"Not mine," he said. "My phone drowned in New Jersey."

The ringing stopped and they decided the sound must have carried through the open window from somewhere in the neighborhood.

"So, no cell phone?" Esther asked pointedly.

"I'll get it replaced this week. Didn't you think it was a little odd that I wasn't checking in?"

"Never noticed," Laura said.

"OK," Russ said. "Hit me with it. What the hell is going on with you two?"

Esther stepped to the desk and came back with the itemized credit card bills. She sat them squarely in front of Russ.

"We weren't intentionally prying," she said. "I just noticed you were in the wrong state for your hurricane."

He glanced at the bills and launched a string of swear words.

"I knew it! I told the police back there to check out that tribe who claimed they had come up from Louisiana to help."

"Tribe?" Laura asked.

"All the volunteers back there lived pretty primitively, but this one group of guys who claimed they had experience with restoration after Hurricane

Katrina just didn't ring true. After the police interviewed them, they all took off back to wherever they had come from. They didn't even stay the rest of the shift," he said.

"They didn't have one carpentry skill among the six of them. They spent most of their time chowing down on the food the feds provided for the volunteers. Every time we needed extra muscle to lift some of the framing, Team Louisiana seemed to evaporate."

"What doesn't ring true," Laura said, "is that you didn't think to borrow a phone and call collect, buy a phone at Walmart, or find one phone booth in all of New Jersey."

"Can we talk about that later?" Russ asked.

He tried to explain that his lost cell phone was due to his own clumsiness, when he slipped on a submerged beam and dropped the phone into the water. Most of the volunteers had been through the drill before and were smart enough not to bring cell phones to a flood restoration project, he added. Laura was listening, but not convinced.

The day after he lost the phone, Russ said, he and several other men who were volunteering had wallets, watches, and other valuables stolen from the makeshift dormitory where they were staying. They had reported the thefts to the authorities, but were more intent on working than on checking in regularly to see if the police had tracked down the Shreveport Six.

"Damn!" he repeated. "How much did they charge?"

"Over two thousand dollars so far," Esther said. "It's not the amount so much as where we thought you were using the card."

Russ looked at the statement again.

"Did you see the strange names of these businesses?" he asked. "And, here's proof it wasn't me using the card. These places are in New York City and Louisiana."

Laura still looked doubtful.

"So I spent close to a month working 5 a.m. until dark, seven days a week, and you both thought I was in Louisiana."

"At strip clubs," Laura said. "Look again."

Russ shook his head in disbelief.

"It gets better," Laura said. "The Portland police want to interview you about Martinelli's murder," she said. "They found it strange that you left so soon after the body was found."

"You've got to be kidding."

"And another thing," put in Esther. "Charmaigne was badly beaten and you match the description of her attacker."

"Our girl Charmaigne told the cops that you and she were a hot item," Laura said.

"No wonder you didn't want to take my call to let you know I was headed home."

"Let's just say I was less than thrilled to pick up a suspected murderer at the airport," Laura said. "I do have my standards."

It was after 8 p.m., but Russ dialed the Portland Police Bureau anyway to report his return to Oregon and set up an appointment for an interview with Roberts and Anderson the next day. Exhausted as he was, he knew he wouldn't sleep well until he had answered their questions.

"Don't be afraid to paint second-hand wood furniture. The first owner didn't love it enough to keep it."

19

"Before you ladies arrived this morning, a likable young man named Jamen Childers dropped off this envelope," Ernie said. He handed Laura a cream colored envelope with an embossed letter "C" on the flap. She turned it over and saw her name written in a clear, black script that mimicked the embossed typeface on the other side of the envelope.

"Check it for white powder like they do at the White House," Esther advised.

Laura looked mildly amused, but was surprised to find she was now holding the envelope by the top left corner between pinched fingers an arm's length away from her body.

"We're being ridiculous," she said.

Esther took two steps back to join Ernie near the doorway while Laura opened what was a completely normal—if embossed—envelope. A handwritten invitation to Laura was inside.

"Francesca Childers has invited me to join her for lunch at one o'clock this Friday afternoon at her country club," Laura reported. "She adds that the expected attire is 'country club casual.'"

"My vote's for a bullet proof vest in whatever this summer's hot color is," Esther advised.

"I wonder what's on her mind? I'm accepting this invitation, but I think I'll meet her at the restaurant. If it's too uncomfortable, I can always leave early."

THE MAÎTRE D' ESCORTED Laura to a small table near the window overlooking a sweeping green lawn dotted with ponds and fountains. He held her chair for her across the table from Mrs. Childers.

"You're not terribly late," the older woman said.

Laura quickly checked her watch and saw that it was 1:02. She smiled at her lunch companion in what she hoped was a socially acceptable half-smile. She might have been two minutes late, but she knew her whitening tooth paste had done a job that even Francesca Childers would deem acceptable.

"I haven't been here before," Laura said. "It's a beautiful setting."

"It is lovely, isn't it, dear? I called Raoul and asked him to have ingredients for three choices of entrée available for us today."

"How thoughtful of you," Laura managed. She was thinking, "Menus. Have you not heard of menus, woman?"

"They make an amazing pomegranate and acai berry glazed duck breast salad. Our other choices include a wild mushroom spinach lasagna, but, on second thought, that might be much too heavy for today," she said. "There's also the herb-crusted wild salmon with orange fennel sauce. I've had that before and it was adequate."

The waiter appeared out of nowhere. Laura glanced down discreetly to see if he was barefoot or had actually managed to cross the room that quietly while wearing shoes.

Francesca ordered the duck salad, but asked that the chef wait to prepare the entrée for fifteen minutes so they might enjoy their "beverages." Her beverage of choice was a ginger-rosemary lemontini. Laura had never heard of a lemontini. There was no way she was joining this woman in a drink in the early afternoon. She caught herself before blurting out "gimme the adequate fish and a Coke."

"I'd like the wild salmon and a glass of unsweetened iced tea, please," she said instead. The waiter floated noiselessly away.

Before the drinks arrived, Francesca announced the reason for this occasion.

"I've brought you a small gift," she said. She produced a manila folder which had apparently been resting on her lap during the conversation so far. The large diamonds on her hand reflected the light from the window as she passed the folder across the table. Laura also took note of Francesca's freshly done French manicure.

"Before you and your, uh, team, explore exterior color choices for your little project, I thought you might want to see this painting and some photos," Francesca said.

"I'd love to!"

"Now, don't get overly excited. These are photos that I have no use for and might be helpful for you to have," she said. She pulled out three different sets of photos showing the color schemes that had been used since the 1950's. There was also a small water color painting of the house showing the original paint colors.

Laura was thrilled to find the 5 x 7 painting showed a color combination in the same warm hues she had tentatively selected for the outside of the home. There were also photos of the original gardens which Francesca dismissed as "too cumbersome for today's life."

They studied the photos as they sipped their drinks, which Laura noticed had appeared at some time while she was examining one of the black and white shots of the gardens.

"This isn't completely a favor I'm doing for you," Francesca said. "I have a definite color preference, you see."

"Oh."

"Since you haven't given up on the house as I had hoped you might," she said. "Is there any chance you would consider returning the structure to its original color. I much prefer it as it looked when I visited my grandmother there."

Laura hesitated for a minute, pretending to deliberate. She peeked discreetly at the paint sample strips she had tucked in her purse earlier to show Francesca. By coincidence—and some previous Internet research—her own color choices mirrored those Francesca was suggesting.

"Well?" the woman prompted before Laura could speak.

Laura would have to finalize the decision on paint colors by the end of next week anyway, so why not today?

"Mrs. Childers," she said, "I think that is a wonderful idea. We will come as close to the original colors as we can with today's paint formulas."

"Thank you," Francesca said simply. "You may keep the photos. I have no use for them," she repeated.

Their orders and a second drink for Francesca arrived and they ate a quiet meal together. As they were finishing the gourmet food, which Laura admitted trumped the tomato and cheese sandwich she usually packed for lunch, a woman approached them. She was about Francesca's age, well attired, and stood perfectly straight. Laura couldn't help but notice the "trout pout" which signaled that the woman had made one too many trips to the plastic surgeon's office.

Francesca invited the new arrival to join them for dessert and, when the woman accepted, Laura saw her chance for escape. She thanked Mrs. Childers, reached for the folder with the photos, and made her exit. Not as quietly as the waiter, but she tried for grace.

The remaining ladies were debating between Black Forest cheesecake and a cherry vanilla cheesecake with ganache and black cherry compote as Laura slipped out the door.

She stopped at Dairy Queen on the way home and ordered the small hot fudge sundae to go.

"People with Obsessive Compulsive Disorder (OCD) shouldn't buy area rugs with fringe. (You know who you are and you know why.)

20

Laura and Russ met the next morning at the Dreams house. He was impressed with the progress made on the house in his absence.

"How's Ernie working out?" he asked.

"He and all the subcontractors have been wonderful," Laura said. "Can we keep him? Please, Dad, can we keep him?" she begged.

"I'm considering it," he said.

"Oh," she remembered. "Detective Pfeifer says 'hello.'"

"Where did you see *him?*"

"We met at that trendy new place down on the riverfront."

"You went out with him?"

What happened to the get-out-and-see-other-people lecture Russ had given her before he left for the East Coast? He needed to make up his mind.

"No. I just ran into him there. But, honestly . . ."

"So we're going to be honest now?"

"You know," she said, "I can't have this conversation with you right now. Give me a call when you've turned back into a reasonable human being."

She stalked out the door—actually paired glass-paned doors under an elaborate Italianate hood supported by hand-carved brackets—and walked toward the driveway, then veered right and focused straight ahead.

That's when the cement truck hit her.

THE DRIVER SEEMED unaware that anything had happened as he backed out of the driveway and into the street. He drove off at a normal rate of speed as Russ raced to Laura's side.

He gently rolled her over, fearing the worst.

"Damn," she said. "I was hoping we'd make it through another year without a workers' comp claim."

"Mein Gott! Why are you even alive?"

"Better question. Why are we speaking German?"

Laura explained that when the left back side of the truck struck her, she tripped and landed on the rain soaked sod at the edge of the driveway. The first set of wheels went over both of her feet. She'd had time to pull her left foot back before the front wheels arrived.

"I'm not even sure I'm injured," she said.

"Of course you're injured," he said impatiently. "You got run over by a cement truck."

He picked her up and carried her to the front seat of his truck for a trip to the emergency room. Laura would remember later that the scariest part of the whole ordeal was the speed which Russ drove to the medical center. He turned on the truck's flashing warning lights and hit the horn continuously as they rushed to the emergency room entrance.

At the hospital, she was seen immediately. "Hit by cement truck" was apparently a powerful phrase to write on admittance forms. It let her by pass the waiting room entirely.

The diagnosis wasn't grim. One foot was severely bruised, the bones probably having survived by being pushed down into the soft, muddy ground. But, images from the lab had shown two small bones broken across the top of her right foot.

Laura soon sported a bright chartreuse walking cast to protect her foot while it healed. She wondered who chose the fashion colors for casts. Neon green was definitely not this year's color.

Staff at the hospital had followed procedure and notified the police when accident victim Laura arrived.

Laura and Russ were ready to leave when they heard Detective Roberts call her name. He requested that Russ join him in a small consultation room usually reserved for doctors to report to waiting family members of ER patients. Roberts and Russ left Laura seated in the hospital lobby while they talked. Russ returned shortly.

"Laura, they're admitting you," he said to her.

"They're *what?*"

The doctor walked into the lobby, escorted by Detective Roberts.

"That's correct," the doctor said. "I know I told you earlier that you could probably go home with a walking cast, but I've talked with the detective here and he's asked me to reconsider that."

Laura looked from the doctor to the detective to Russ. Each of the three stared back at her.

"I smell a rat," she said.

"I told you she wouldn't buy it," Russ said.

"Quiet," the detective said. "We'd be violating procedures to not follow the recommendations of your physician," he said to Laura.

"My physician? We only met an hour ago in the emergency room," she explained. "Where, I might add, he downplayed the seriousness of the injury. He said I'd be hopping down stairs in no time. Isn't that right?" she asked the doctor.

The doctor looked at the other two men, then mumbled something about being paged and having to get back to work. There was an uneasy silence as the he left the lobby.

"You need to level with her," Russ said. "She's not an idiot."

"She walked in front of a cement truck."

"Tell her," Russ said.

Russ and the detective pulled up folding chairs that had been balanced against the wall, and began speaking in low voices to Laura, trying to convince her of the wisdom of not leaving the hospital.

Roberts checked his cell phone for messages, then took a deep breath, and told Laura what had happened since she and Russ left the construction site for the hospital. The cement truck had been found abandoned three blocks away from the Street of Dreams. The original driver had stumbled down the driveway at the Dreams house about the same time. He was rubbing his scalp where someone had conked him in the back of the head after pulling him out of the driver's seat and leaving him on the muddy ground at the back of the house.

The "assailant," as Roberts called the driver who struck Laura, then jumped in the truck and intentionally backed the truck toward Laura as he descended the driveway.

"In short," Roberts said. "This wasn't an accident."

"Yes it was. I was annoyed at Russ and not watching where I was going."

"And, the guy driving the truck was watching you and adjusting his aim as he approached. He had more than enough time to bring that truck to a stop. Estimates are he was only going ten miles per hour until he saw you. Then he sped up."

"He was trying to hit me?" she asked incredulously.

"That's what we're telling you," Russ said. "It wasn't the regular driver. Some guy hijacked that oversized truck and aimed it right at you."

"It wasn't an accident?" she asked again.

"It wasn't an accident," he repeated.

'You're in trouble here," Roberts said.

"Oh, shoot," she said.

"Close," the detective said.

While Laura could handle being in an accident, being the victim an attempted hit and squish had a whole different ring to it.

"But, my foot is OK?" she asked.

"Your foot's going to be OK," the detective said. "Your life's in danger."

AFTER A BRIEF NEGOTIATION Laura convinced the others that she would be safe staying with Esther for a few days. The men had been unyielding until Laura played her last card:

"Our insurance company won't cover days spent in the hospital for a hideout," she said. "Esther will accept me without verification of insurance, ID, or anything. And, she'll feed me really well."

Laura admitted to herself—and later to Esther—that she was frightened.

"Remember when I said I wasn't going to 'do scared' again?" she asked Esther. "Well, I was wrong. Dead wrong."

"It hasn't been a picnic, these past few weeks," Esther pointed out. "Who thought we'd be on first name basis with this many cops?"

"What if someone does want us to abandon the Italianate house after all this work?" Laura asked. "And why would they want us out? They'd have to have a really big reason to kill some guy and then beat up Charmaigne."

"What if you were supposed to be the victim instead of Charmaigne?" Esther pondered.

"I found her on the back porch in daylight. I can't imagine anyone confusing the two of us."

"Not a chance this side of hell," Esther said.

"Until the cement truck hit me," Laura said looking down at her colorful footwear, "I thought the recent events were unusual, but not necessarily aimed at Graham Construction."

"The back of that truck was pointed dead-center, directly at you," Russ reminded her as he entered.

"Well, that little cheerful tidbit certainly eases my fears."

"It's always possible that none of these things are related," Esther said. "Maybe Martinelli, Charmaigne and you were the victims of unrelated industrial accidents."

"Do you believe that?" Laura asked.

"Nope."

"Apparently neither does OSHA or they'd have people crawling all over the site by now," Russ said.

"Now, that's a happy thought."

CHARMAIGNE WAS waiting at the construction site when Laura arrived the next day.

"Have the cops found out anything new about Handy Andy?" Charmaigne asked.

"Who's Handy Andy?" Laura asked.

"You know. The guy under the cement. I can never remember his name."

"It's Salvador Martinelli. And, if they've found out anything new, they haven't bothered to tell me about it," Laura said. "Why do you ask?"

"Because it's so creepy," Charmaigne answered. "I don't know how you can go to sleep at night without thinking about it."

"I've been sleeping well again lately," Laura said, "but I imagine that just ended since you brought the subject up again."

"It's just so creepy. If you know what I mean . . ."

"The quatrefoil is giving the fleur-de-lis a run for its euros on the decorating scene. The Greek Key is still the key to jazzing up plain linens or draperies."

21

The plumber was already at work in the downstairs bathroom when Laura arrived at the Dream site. He helped her move a steadier ladder down the central staircase. She had a favorite blue and yellow hard resin and metal step ladder that she used for painting and wallpapering jobs, but this job required that she be higher up and surer of foot. Singular. The broken bones in her right foot were still mending. She was mobile, but not yet nimble.

She was in the downstairs "side room" which she thought the original owners used as a library. The room's beautiful double windows had been boarded up from the outside when Laura first saw the house. Now the sunlight streamed in. On the outside wall there was a mellowed natural brick fireplace, which Graham Construction planned to close off and use for "purely decorative purposes." (An expression made popular by realtors who didn't want to answer "so sad, too bad" when asked if a fireplace was operative.)

She steadied the ladder and held the large framed oil painting high in front of her as she moved up the rungs, using her elbows for balance as she climbed. She leaned forward to place the painting on the carved mahogany mantel piece and against the wall. She paused and steadied herself. She heard a loud, rumbling sound, and dust rose up from the floor, surrounding her and blocking the lower rungs of the ladder from sight.

The ladder wobbled. Bricks tumbled into the room and she yelled for help. The plumber, who had heard the roar, was coming through the door to investigate. He steadied the ladder with strong hands and helped her down. They both backed across the room to survey the damage from a safe distance.

"What the 'H' happened?" Laura asked.

Plumber Joe Clarke didn't answer instantly. He thought it would sound flippant to tell her they'd have to wait until the dust settled.

When the dust did stop swirling, they both inspected the mess. The brickwork on the back of the fireplace had given way and fallen into the room, causing some of the chimney brick above to follow.

The landscape painting Laura had been auditioning for a place above the mantle was on the floor, now half buried by bricks.

They cleared away the fallen brick and chunks of old mortar and inspected the bricks that were still in place.

"I was sure we'd be looking at brick saturation," Joe Clarke said. "But, there's no indication of that."

"Other than the obvious, what does 'brick saturation' mean?" Laura asked.

"In a wet climate, bricks can chip from freezing conditions and heavy hail. Or, they become saturated from all the rain," he said. "But, if that were the case, the inspector would have found evidence of leakage up where the chimney passes through the attic."

"Oh." It was the best Laura could do to further the conversation. They finished sweeping the brick aside, and she breathed a sigh of relief that the old hardwood flooring had not yet been sanded and refinished. She surveyed the scrapes and gouges the falling bricks had made in the wood when they hit the floor.

"I can't tell whether you had cracked and deteriorating mortar here or if the support pins used to hold the fireplace gave way."

Laura turned to thank him for the rescue, but Clarke had now climbed almost completely into the firebox and was inspecting the mortar between the bricks that were still standing.

"Look at this," he said.

All Laura saw was the stained inside of a hundred-and-some-year old fireplace.

"Look at the mortar between the remaining bricks," he said. "It's not worn away or deteriorating in a crumbling manner like you'd expect. It almost looks like it has been scraped away in this one area."

"Why would anybody do that?" Laura asked.

"Beats me. It looks like something sharp has been run along the mortar holding the bricks on the outer wall of the fireplace box."

"Do you suppose a squirrel or raccoon got trapped in the fireplace at some time through the years?" she asked.

"Anything's possible, I suppose," he said. "But, how would an animal know to try to knock out a brick to get back to the yard? Did you find an old carcass in here?"

"The initial cleanup was done before I saw the house for the first time."

Clarke returned to his plumbing job and Laura reminded herself that the fireplace in this room was going to be closed off anyway. She saw that the sconces were now layered in dust and the top of the painting looked like it had been through a recent snow fall, covered all along the upper edge with a soft white powder.

Clarke poked his head around the door frame. "I should have asked earlier. Are you OK?"

"Dusty, but OK."

"If those bricks had hit the ladder with any more force, you'd have landed on the floor," he said. "That's a good way to break a hip."

"Thanks. I'm OK," she repeated.

"You're limping," he pointed out.

"No worries. I was hit by a cement truck."

Joe Clarke quietly stepped out of the room, shaking his head.

THINGS WERE STILL cool between Laura and Russ, but they kept with the routine of joining Esther for lunch a couple of times a week so they could coordinate their individual parts of the project and keep the building materials they had ordered arriving no more than two days before they were needed. Since the economic downturn, contractors throughout the state knew better than to leave portable tools, equipment and costly supplies stacked outside at a building site unguarded overnight.

The one thing Laura and Russ could agree on was that, while Ward Simmons may have been a poor excuse for a security guard, his presence might protect Russ' investment in tools.

Laura knew she had to report this morning's fireplace collapse to Russ so he could check the fireplace—or what remained of it—before day's end. But, she didn't want to lead with that information. She waited until he had devoured half a sandwich.

"It did what?" he yelled.

She explained the fireplace calamity calmly, but Russ only heard the sound of the danger that had surrounded her. Laura, on the other hand, thought she'd done an admirable job of not mentioning that she was hanging from the top of that ladder when the bricks had started falling into the room and bouncing against the bottom rungs.

"Do you have these near-death experiences just to raise my cardio rate?"

"Lower your voice," she said. "You're turning into Yelling Russ."

"I'm not yelling," he said lowering the volume slightly. "I'm scared to death that you're turning into a liability."

"Oh, so now I'm an insurance rate raiser, am I? Quick! Where's the Geico gecko?"

"Time out!" Esther said, using her hands like a football referee. "From my point of view, Laura is reporting some possible vandalism to the house. And," she said looking directly at Russ, "you, Russ, are expressing your concern that she was in danger."

"Again," he added.

"So, truce," Esther said.

Esther left the room and Laura lowered her voice so she could be heard by only Russ.

"Sometimes I wonder about us," Laura said.

"That's what I needed time to think about. I needed time away from here and seeing each other every day. It's why I forced myself to stay out of touch."

"You needed three weeks?"

He caught her off guard when he answered.

"I needed only one day away to know that you're the one. I just about went crazy without you back there. I needed to know for sure," he said. "I didn't want to be another man making your life miserable."

"No one could top Todd Howard in that department."

"Thank you, I think."

"Could we rewind this conversation," Laura asked.

"We could if you still had an old-fashioned tape recorder lying around," he said.

"I want to go back to 'you're the one.'"

He took her hand in his and said, "It's not a hard concept, Love."

"Then, you didn't leave town to get away from me?"

"Good grief! Is that what you thought?" he asked. "I just saw an opportunity to do some good and also give myself some time to think things out."

"Oh."

"I love you. I think I've always loved you," he corrected himself. "But, it's important to me that I don't end up disappointing you like Todd did."

"Are you a liar, a cheat, and a fraud?"

"Of course not," he said, slightly offended.

"Then, I think we're OK."

"We're better than OK," he said.

LAURA ANSWERED the phone at The Harrington the next morning and recognized Detective Robert's voice. He was calling about her recent run in—or run over—with the cement truck.

"We're still measuring the crime scene and trying to re-enact the accident, Ms. Howard. I have a few more questions to ask you," Detective Roberts said.

"Shoot."

"I beg your pardon," the Detective said.

"Poor choice of words," Laura said. "I meant 'go ahead. Ask away.'"

"Our questions concern the direction you were running. In my experience, most people leaving the house in a rush, as you said you were, would run directly to the street. Agreed?"

"I suppose so," Laura said.

"But, if we've reconstructed the scene correctly, you ran in an arc pattern," he said. "Could you help me with why that would have happened?"

"I never walk across the cement area where Mr. Martinelli was found."

"Would you think to avoid that area even when you were as angry as you reported you were that day?"

"Wouldn't you?"

"I'm asking you, Ms. Howard."

"I haven't stepped foot on that part of the yard since the day I found the hand."

"You'd think about that even when you were running?"

"I think about that every day. Finding dead people may be in your job description, Detective, but it's a once-in-a-life-time event for me. I hope," she added.

"Right. Right. OK, I was just checking," he said.

"Call any time," she said and hung up.

"One huge piece of wall art trumps seven little ones."

22

"The ladies," as Ernie always called them, had gone out to lunch today and Ernie was trying to catch up on some work during what should have been his lunch hour. It was the constant interruptions that made this job different from others in his past.

"If it wasn't ditzy Charmaigne, it was Edward Simmons at the door," Ernie thought as he heard yet another knock at the front entrance. He stopped work and went to the porch to see if he could keep Simmons from coming inside and delaying the tiling job until the grout wasn't workable.

"Have you come across a homeless guy here early mornings?" Simmons asked. "He seemed harmless enough, but he wouldn't give me his name last night. He did leave when I told him to go."

"I think I know the guy you mean. Esther Graham calls him Harmless Homeless."

"That's his name?"

"No," Ernie said. "That's how we think of the old guy. I had to point out the Porta-Potty to him once, but, otherwise, he hasn't caused any problems around here."

"Then you don't want me to send him packing?"

"I'll check with Laura and Esther, but I hate to hassle a guy who's down on his luck. Last time I saw him, he had a half a bag of bread someone had given him and, I'm afraid, that was Homeless' entire dinner," Ernie said. "Once in a while, I slip him a few dollars for food or bring him a bag of fruit from home."

"That's a big mistake," Simmons said. "There's no point in encouraging a bum like that."

"There but by the grace of God . . ." Ernie said as he headed back to his tiling chore. If he was lucky, the grout would still be workable.

"LAURA," PFEIFER'S MESSAGE on her cell phone started, "we've had a call from Esther. The officer at the front desk took the call and found it quite threatening. I think I've convinced him that Esther is disgruntled and frustrated by the lack of progress on the case and not a danger to the community. I want to get this cooled down right away. Could you give me a call when you get a chance?"

"Esther!" Laura called out when she climbed the stairs to the back door of the apartment built over the Graham Construction workshop.

She heard no reply.

"Esther," Laura called again at the back door of Esther's apartment. "I know you're in there."

Esther came forward and unlatched the screen door to let Laura inside. She was carrying a goldfish in a miniature net balanced over a small clear bowl of fresh water.

"Is there anything you want to tell me about?" Laura asked.

"Not really," the older woman said.

"How about threatening someone at the other end of the phone when you called the Police Bureau earlier today?"

"I wasn't threatening. I was assertive. There's a difference," Esther said. "The guy was uncooperative."

"He was doing his job," Laura said.

"Not really. He refused to answer anything I asked him."

"Chances are pretty good that the guy at the front desk wouldn't have information about cases."

"I didn't think of that," Esther said.

"Did it occur to you that the man's credibility—and possibly his job—would be in danger if he divulged the progress on cases to anonymous callers?"

"I've got my own 'street cred' to protect," Esther said. "If they'd tell me what they've found out so far, I could help solve this case."

Laura recalled that Esther had provided the final piece of the puzzle surrounding Todd Howard's death, but she doubted that this qualified Esther to butt into an open and on-going police investigation. Unfortunately, Pfeifer himself had asked Esther at the time of Todd's death if she had ever considered a career in police work. A little praise apparently lingered for a long time where Esther was concerned.

Laura was going to say more, but Esther was now busy returning the fish to bowl.

"Mona," Esther said to the fish, "don't take any crap in life."

LAURA CALLED PFEIFER to let him know that Esther would not be harassing the front desk person again. She had her fingers crossed when she said it, but it was as close to a promise as she could make where Esther was involved.

"We both know, I'm fond of your Aunt Esther," he said. "But could you keep a damper on her when she's dealing with other officers?"

"Her main concern," Laura explained, "was that we haven't heard any progress on the case. She claims TV detectives are able to solve cases in an hour-long show and that includes time out for commercials."

Pfeifer groaned. "Just do your best. It'll be hard for me to get it reversed if she gets herself arrested for menacing."

"I'll try," Laura said, "but, you might remind your guys that, where Esther's concerned, 'fire crackers come in small packages.'"

"Nothing known to man removes burn marks from firecrackers or sparklers landing on cement patios. Remember that pot of geraniums at the end of Chapter 16?"

23

Laura woke from another nightmare and sat straight up in bed, trying to see where she was and calm her racing heart.

Louise meowed loudly, then climbed across Laura's legs and moved up the bed to rub his soft orange fur against her shoulder.

"It's OK," Laura said. "We're at The Harrington. We're safe."

The cat apparently agreed because he settled in the crook of Laura's arm and began to knead his paws in the knit coverlet on the bed.

When Laura got to work in the morning, she pulled Esther aside.

"What do you know about the meaning of dreams?" she asked Esther.

"Not a thing. Oh, wait. I think dreams about falling are about insecurity or anxiety. Why do you ask?"

"It's Martinelli again," Laura said.

"You're going to worry yourself to death."

"The dream wasn't about death. His or mine," she said. "In the dream, Todd and I were at our wedding, but when I slid the gold wedding band on his hand, his fingers were caked with dried cement."

"A psychologist would have a field day with you," Esther said.

"I don't need a shrink. I need the police to solve this case so I can relax and have my old life back again."

"That would be the life where you were married to a cheater, lived in a one-bedroom apartment on the wrong side of town, and were shot at in Seaside?" Esther asked.

"Well, when you put it that way, my old life did have its drawbacks," Laura concluded.

THE NEXT NIGHT Laura heard Pfeifer walking up the stone path to the door of The Harrington. He had called around 9 p.m. to say there had been "new developments" and he'd be stopping by to see her tomorrow morning. Apparently he had changed his mind.

"Come in, come in," Laura said. "Why do I feel like I should sit down to hear this news?"

"Why do *I* feel like you should put on a bathrobe?"

Laura glanced down at her light summer nightgown and reached for a raincoat from the coat closet near the entryway at The Harrington.

"Sorry," she said.

"You can't answer the door in the middle of the night dressed like that."

Laura had been half asleep with a copy of *House Beautiful* still in her hands before she heard the footsteps and the doorbell rang. Louise jumped on the couch to announce they had guests, emphasizing the importance of his message by swiping his front paw across her face. When Laura peered at the street through a slit between the draperies, she saw a police car parked in front of the house. It was shortly after 10 p.m.

"You're right. I should be more careful," she said to Pfeifer as she showed him to the living room. "I didn't think any other cop would stop by this late."

"Wrong. We're available 24 hours a day. 'Sworn to protect and dedicated to serve,'" he said.

"Right."

"I should have called a second time," he said more seriously. "This is an official call. There's been a problem over at your building site."

"Story of my life on this project," she said. "What now? Broken water pipe? Wind blew the shingles off? Kids tagged it with graffiti?"

"Worse," he said. "There was a fire. The house. . . "

"Burned to the ground! I knew this was next," she interrupted.

"No. Listen," he commanded. "Listen. Very carefully, please."

"OK. I'm ready."

"There was a fire," he repeated. "The fire started in the carriage house out back and travelled across to the railing of the long back porch."

"But, how?

"I'm going to keep talking," Pfeifer said. "Your job is to keep quiet and listen. If I forget and pause, don't fill in the air time."

Laura nodded.

"Do you know if anyone was living in the carriage house?" Pfeifer asked.

The room was quiet.

"Do you know if anyone was staying back there?" he asked again. He looked at Laura expectantly.

"I can't both follow your directions and answer that," she said. "No one was living there," she continued. "But, all of Russ' expensive tools were stored in there along with any supplies we had on hand. That's why we kept the place padlocked."

"We're only in the preliminary stages of the investigation, but it looks like someone had clearly breached your padlock security system."

"How can you tell if the house burned to the ground?"

"Forget 'burned to the ground.' *You* said that. I didn't," he reminded her.

"Oh."

"The primary structure was saved. The back porch was damaged, but the fire department concentrated on keeping the roof on the main house wet and let the smaller structure burn itself out. The back building was engulfed when the fire department got there."

"So, it's only 'burned to the ground' where the carriage house is concerned," Laura said. "The house is mostly OK," she verified. "That's not so bad, I guess."

"It gets worse," he said. "The main house was saved, but someone was in the carriage house at the time of the blaze and didn't make it out."

"Like tripped and broke a leg on the way out? Or, like didn't make it out and died?"

"Perished," he said. "Burned beyond recognition, I'm afraid."

Pfeifer explained that he had come to make sure she wasn't the victim.

"Now, there was a frightening idea," she thought as she continued to fight her gag reflex.

Pfeifer wanted to be with her when she called Esther and Russ to make sure neither of them had stopped by the property late at night. He also needed to ask her if there was anyone else who would have had legitimate business at the Dreams house at that hour.

It took less than a minute to verify that the Grahams were OK, tucked safely in their beds up the block. The event was still tragic for someone's family, but Laura's friends were safe. And, Russ knew that Ernie had left town for the weekend to see his grandkids who lived in Astoria.

"You'll need to call your insurance carrier first thing in the morning," Pfeifer said. "We can't give their people access to the property, though, until our own investigation is over and the state arson team is out of there."

"You think it was intentionally set?" she asked.

"There was a burned gas can near the victim's remains. That's considered a darn good sign."

"Is there any chance the victim was one of the other builders on the street?" Laura asked.

"Will Anderson is down at the Bureau right now, contacting each of them by phone. I think he'd have called by now if he had been unable to reach any of them. He had all the contact info from the Martinelli case."

Pfeifer's cell phone rang and he pulled it from the black leather pouch and listened to it for five minutes.

"That was Anderson," he said. "All the builders and all their people are accounted for. Our guys at the scene have already established that it was arson and it looks like the perpetrator planned on seeing the whole thing go up in smoke."

"How can they tell that?" Laura asked.

"There were two more gas cans hidden out behind the trees in the side yard."

"Why would anyone do that?" she asked.

"There's usually either a motive of revenge or insurance fraud behind crimes of arson. With juvenile perpetrators, the crime often ties to a history of sexual abuse," he explained.

THE NEXT MORNING, Pfeifer called Laura and asked if she, Russ and Esther could drop by the Police Bureau in the early afternoon. He had what he called "some grim news" to report about the fire victim at the Dreams Street house. Esther drove and despite Russ' fears for their safety, they arrived in time for the meeting.

"Before we get going here," Esther asked, "do any of us need an attorney?"

"I wouldn't think so," Pfeifer said. "The victim was a 27-year-old woman who mostly lived on the streets in Burnside and parts of East Portland. She has several prior arrests for soliciting over the past eight years, four DUII's, plus a breaking and entering charge on her juvenile record."

"I thought juvenile records were sealed at age 21," Esther said. Laura and Russ both turned to look at her, each wondering why she would know that.

"It's 18, and they are," Pfeifer said. "But, if it helps solve a homicide, we can request that information. In those cases, the earlier record will no longer taint the victim's adult life and it might help us find a killer."

The four sat uncomfortably on city-issue straight back chairs, waiting to see who would speak first. Pfeifer took the lead.

"The deceased was Maria Teresa Salazar, dob 11-19, no distinguishing scars, tattoos, or piercings discernible when the body was recovered. Apparently no relatives in the area, no permanent address," he concluded. "No one has inquired about the body," he added.

"Did she burn to death or was she dead when the fire started?" Esther asked bluntly.

"We believe, Mrs. Graham, that she was the only one on the site at the time of the blaze. A blood toxicology test would be virtually impossible, but we suspect she could have been intoxicated at the time."

"So," Esther said. "You want to know which one of us hangs with a drunken prostitute who wanted to take revenge on a defenseless old house."

"I wouldn't have put it quite like that."

"I'm out," Esther said. "How 'bout you Russ and you, Laura?"

They each shook their heads "no."

Pfeifer sat there slack-jawed for thirty seconds, wondering if he had ever met anyone as efficient at getting to the point as Esther Graham.

He turned to Esther to explain how they'd been able to identify Salazar. They'd bypassed DNA testing, first trying forensic dental identification. Based on the victim's lifestyle, Pfeifer had contacted Medical Teams International, which provides a dental van in

Multnomah County and hosts free dental clinics locally for those with no insurance and no reasonable means of paying for dental care, he explained.

"The group doesn't provide routine exams," Pfeifer said, "but serves those with urgent dental needs. It turns out the medical team had pulled two teeth and restored a third for the victim in December 2012. No charge."

"There's room in every house for somber colors."

24

The insurance agent looked at the site after the fire and, while he couldn't make any promises on how quickly the main office would act to cut a check for the losses from the fire, he did understand the urgency of replacing the tools Russ had collected over a period of years. It wasn't the sort of investment that could be easily replaced with one quick trip to a hardware store.

Those tools were Graham Construction's livelihood. This most recent event was going to set Russ even farther back from the completion date he had set and could very well prevent Graham Construction from having a finished product to show at the open house. Russ wondered if that was the culprit's goal.

He was surveying the damage when Gary Young, the contractor building the house next door, walked over.

"I hope your insurance company understands that a man's tools are more than just implements from the hardware store," he said. "Why I've got one hammer that has been on my belt for over twenty years. And, I know you guys all laugh at it, but Big Red, my favorite shovel, is more dependable than many of my friends."

Russ did understand. He hadn't ever had another builder admit the bond between a man and his tools, but he definitely felt the loss of more than metal and steel.

"This is the key to the tool shed at the back of my lot next door," Gary said. "I want you to feel free to come and go as you like, borrow anything you need night or day."

Russ didn't quite know what to say, but managed a meek "Thank you." He had misjudged Gary Young. Russ had mistaken the man's silence through the last few months as lack of friendliness when, in truth, the guy was as busy as the rest of them trying to meet the completion deadline. Gary was generous to a fault, Russ now realized, and he must be the most patient man on earth if he was able to work with Charmaigne daily. Maybe by the time he'd spent five days a week with the woman, the man had been "talked out."

RUSS AND HAMMER came in the side door at Graham Construction where Esther greeted them with a cup of coffee and a dog biscuit.

"Take your pick," she said to Russ.

He sipped the hot strong coffee appreciatively, glancing around the downstairs room and listening for any sign that Laura had arrived at work before him.

"No Laura?" he asked.

"She's out at the site," Esther answered. "Making lemonade."

"Not that anything surprises me about Laura, but why is she out there?"

"Like I said. She's trying to see the good side of having the carriage house gone and now having all that space to design a patio, outside eating area, and Italian gardens."

"Italian gardens?"

"Probably not a big crop: garlic, oregano, onions, tomatoes."

"I think I'll drive out and see for myself," he said. He whistled for Hammer to join him and the two drove out to the site where, true enough, Laura was wandering around the area behind the house. The burnt remnants of the carriage house had been bulldozed and pushed aside

"I'm trying to look at this as an opportunity instead of a tragedy," she told Russ. "I loved the idea of the carriage house turned into an artist's studio, but it did limit the number of buyers who might have been interested."

"Hmmm. You saw that old building as an artist's retreat?" he asked. "I saw it remodeled as a man cave with big screen entertainment."

"Well, in order to cut expenses, I'm now trying to see this spot as an Italianate courtyard with multiple container gardens. The whole thing could be surrounded by arched entryways. In my eye, it has a small reflecting pool, a flagstone patio area with World Market outdoor furniture, and a small shelter to store those wrought iron furniture pieces during the rainy season."

"The idea has some appeal if we're still trying to keep to our original timeline," he said. "In fact, if I only have to replace the porch, we might actually be back on schedule."

"That was my thought, too," she said. "We may save more days than dollars, though, if I don't restrain myself from picturing stucco arched openings on four sides."

"You wouldn't need one on the house side," he pointed out.

"And I suppose I could use boxwood in groomed hedges along two sides."

"See? You're down to one archway already."

"One, amazing, knock-your-eyes-out archway," she said.

"I have just three words," he responded. "Budget, budget, and budget."

She moved toward the side of the house to pick up the sketch book she had stashed there and Russ called over his shoulder.

"What happened to the vegetables?" he asked.

"Vegetables?"

"Never mind," he said. He didn't want to admit that Esther's earlier teasing had gone right over his head again. He had accepted early in life that women spoke a different language than men. But Esther and Laura were quicker than he could keep up with most days.

He wandered over to inspect the singed siding on the back of the house and the charred porch railing. His restoration plans were simpler than Laura's visions for the garden. The porch would be replaced with a replica of the original. He would put skid free paint on the porch floor boards, but other than that, it would be like the first one. Only sturdier.

"And, that," he told Hammer, "is why we need Laura around for the creative part."

Hammer gave a single bark.

"Right." Russ said.

THERE WERE SOME places where Laura could wander day in and day out without ever getting bored. Plant nurseries were at the top of the list, followed closely by open air flea markets and wholesale yardage stores. And don't ever let her loose in Pier One.

It was worth the trip to Garland's Nursery northeast of Corvallis to look for the right garden statue. The plan was to have the statue visible through the arch that would welcome visitors.

Unfortunately, so far she was finding mainly statues of aquatic animals or forest creatures. Then she saw it.

191

A gracefully sculpted young woman with her long skirts blowing in the wind and carrying a stone garden basket full of carefully crafted clay wild flowers. The art work took Laura's breath away.

It was old-fashioned without looking out of date. It was traditional without being kitsch. It was twice her budget.

"She's worth every penny," Laura said to no one in particular. She could alter some of the other costs by changing her selection of perennials for the flower beds in which the stone woman would stand.

There was no title on the work. Laura knew the statue would need a name if she was to join them in the Italianate garden. She decided to call the woman Vivian.

Laura didn't attempt to lift the statue, but found a young man in a hunter green nursery apron who was willing to first heft "Vivian" onto an open nursery wagon, then wrap the statue in used burlap sacks, and transport her carefully to Laura's truck bed.

As he wrapped Vivian for safe travel, Laura noticed the single word ITALY stamped on the bottom of the left foot of the statue. Now she knew she had made the right selection. She definitely had not heard any news reports of China's economy going belly-up since she started her one woman anti-made-in-China campaign last year, but she felt pleased each time she could make the tiniest dent in sales of Asian imports.

Laura took the back road through Aumsville to Portland to keep her new friend Vivian safe from sudden stops and potential accidents on I-5.

The 120-mile round trip to Corvallis was well worth the trouble, but she'd abide by the Chamber of Commerce advice and "shop local" for the ferns and small variety rhododendrons she needed for the shade gardens. She wanted the statue to look at home in her outdoor environment, not like she had been planted there as an afterthought.

The area behind the Italianate house would be primarily a hardscape of flagstone and river rock, with several well-mulched areas left for shade plants. The height of the house cast shadows except for about a two-hour stretch in the late afternoon. The statue of the young woman would be placed carefully so she could be seen looking at her reflection in the small pool as visitors entered the garden. Vivian was barefoot, Laura noted, but her feet would soon be covered with periwinkle to keep them warm year round.

The nursery employee had surrounded the statue with the few plants Laura had selected for now and helped her secure a blue plastic tarp over the truck bed. It was amazing what she had learned by reading the gardening book she had borrowed from Jamen Childers. There was a long list of other plants to buy yet. She'd need ferns of every variety along with bleeding hearts, forget-me-nots, hostas, daisies, violets, and some winter hazel.

Then, of course, she'd have to introduce Vivian to Russ and Esther.

AFTER A WEEK of planting, Laura was ready to unveil the gardens and back patio to Russ and Esther. The reflecting pool was complete and the pump functioning quietly. The statue was surrounded by low-growing perennials that would thrive in the shady area. The arch had been completed last week. It was time for Esther and Russ to see the results. Ernie had been allowed to follow the process of the garden restoration day by day, but it had been off limits to Russ and Esther.

The three of them came around from the west side of the house and approached the arch that had taken Laura days to design. They stopped abruptly when they thought they saw someone standing in the backyard Framed in the archway was a woman wearing what looked like Laura's color-splattered painting clothes. As they got closer, they gasped in unison.

"They've beheaded Vivian," Laura wailed.

Russ motioned the women to stay back and rushed forward to find that his expected victim was a concrete statue.

"Come on in," he said in a relieved voice. "It's someone's idea of a joke."

"It's no joke," Laura said. "That's—or was—Vivian."

"Why was she wearing your clothes?"

"Where's her head?" Laura asked in disbelief.

Russ surveyed the yard but came back without the missing head. Laura was angrier than the other two could ever remember seeing her.

"It's vandalism and we should report it," Esther said.

"Can you call the nursery and get another statue?" Russ asked.

"No. She was the only one. And, something else wouldn't be the same."

"Could the sculptor duplicate it?"

"I wouldn't know where to start to look for him."

"There can't be that many statues named Vivian," he said.

"You don't get it. *I* called her Vivian. The artist hadn't bothered to name her."

As Laura began to delicately remove Vivian's work clothes, Charmaigne called out to them from the yard next door.

"What's she going on about this time?" Esther asked.

"Probably a spider," Laura said.

Russ walked over to the building site next door and came back with a funny look on his face.

"Look up," he said.

Neither woman saw anything.

"Look at the chimney on Charmaigne and Gary's house. Someone has replaced the chimney cap with what I suspect is your friend Vivian's head."

Their eyes followed the brickwork up to the roof of the structure.

"This is really sick," Esther said.

"And, not easy to do in the middle of the night without an extension ladder," Russ added.

"What did Viv ever do to anyone?" Laura asked.

"I don't know," Russ said, "but I know what we're going to do. Don't touch anything. I'm calling the police. The whole scene is finally creeping me out."

"MS. HOWARD," the officer said.

"Laura," she corrected Officer Carter who had been on patrol in the area when the call came in.

"Ma'am."

Russ quickly stepped in front of Laura, holding his finger to his lips to shush the cop.

"Laura," he said. "This is Officer Carter." He looked back to the officer. "Sir, this is *Laura Howard.*" Russ hoped he had averted a predictable outburst from Laura and they could get down to business. He might have to make a sign declaring this as a "No Ma'am Zone" before the summer was over, but for now they could proceed.

"Let's start with the easy questions," Carter said. "When did the statue get here?"

"I brought her home a week ago," Laura said.

"And where had it been before?"

"Don't call her 'it.' Her name was Vivian."

"Okaaaay," he said. "Where did your concrete friend here reside last?"

"In Corvallis at a plant nursery."

"And, did Viv seem happy here?" he asked.

"Stop it! I'm not a nut case," Laura said. "I was fond of the statue is all. And, she was expensive."

"What do you estimate the loss figure to be?"

Laura winced.

"As she is now or as she was?"

"What did you pay for her?" he asked.

"One thousand three hundred and seventy nine dollars," she said. "More or less."

She heard Russ inhale sharply

"This crime passed 'petty theft' $1,279 ago," Carter said. "I'm going to run this address and see if there have been any other thievery or vandalism incidents in the neighborhood."

"We can probably save you some time," Esther said. "I'd start by calling Detective Leonard Roberts and asking him about the Sal Martinelli case and any cases on file on this street since then."

The officer returned to his car and remained there with a cell phone at his ear for some time. When he came back, he was much more serious.

"Roberts believes someone is intentionally harassing and directly threatening you," Carter said.

"I've heard that before," Laura answered.

"You may have heard the warning," he said, "but why haven't you heeded it?"

"What more can I do? I'm only here daylight hours when Ernie, Russ or Esther are on site too. I took interior photos of the rooms so I wouldn't be tempted to swing by on weekends and re-measure anything.

There are two more people less than 50 feet away at the next building site."

"Where do you park your vehicle?"

"Usually out front," she said.

"You need to be more careful. Park your vehicle where you can see it while you work. All kinds of things could happen to it if someone's threatening you," he said. "I'll check it for explosives and inspect the brakes before I leave," Carter said.

"You've got to be kidding."

"No," he said. "You've got to accept that this is no joke," he said. "I've got all I need here for now. We'll increase the patrols up here tonight," he said.

"Thank you."

"If you can get your little pal's head out of the brickwork, someone might be able to repair her," he added as an afterthought.

Russ thanked the officer for his time and the three of them were left standing beside the maimed statue. The remark about the explosives had sobered Laura, but she still stared at what was left of Vivian.

"Maybe she could wear a scarf," Russ suggested quietly.

"Aqua chiffon for Easter," Esther added.

"Refresh a wilting bouquet from the florists by adding greenery from your yard—or your neighbor's yard after dark."

25

Everyone on the Graham team was exhausted when they headed home from work at 6 p.m. Friday. They looked forward to the weekend. Laura talked of a daytrip to the coast for Saturday. Russ thought he'd take in a Portland Timbers game and then get some rest before returning to the worksite Monday morning. Ernie didn't share his plans.

Esther surprised them all when she announced that she planned to redeem a gift certificate for a spa day Saturday in Lake Oswego before the certificate expired in her kitchen drawer.

LAURA HAD BEEN at odds all Friday evening. She walked up the block to see if Esther would like some company. Esther wasn't home, but Laura knew she often sneaked out in the early evening to get a fresh strawberry milkshake at the nearby Burgerville. She noticed Russ' truck was gone, too, and decided he had probably stopped off for a beer with some of the other builders.

She wasn't that sorry to find that they were both away from home. Now she could return to The Harrington and feel no guilt as she tucked in early with a good book and Louise curled up at the foot of the bed.

"I BLEW THAT ONE," Russ said to the dog who greeted him at the door when he returned to Graham Construction late Friday night. Hammer didn't seem particularly interested in extending the conversation and wandered into the kitchen to hint that he was hungry.

"Hammer, old friend, I'll feed you in a couple of minutes. I want to catch Laura before she leaves." Russ dialed, but there was no answer at Laura's place. He didn't want to leave a message.

The dog was now sitting by the cupboard where Russ kept the large bag of dog chow, gently using his paws to try to open the door. Russ helped him out by pouring some dry food in a metal bowl and topping it off with some left-over gravy he had stored in the refrigerator from dinner the night before. "Sorry," he said to the dog as he sat the bowl down on the floor. "I didn't mean to make you wait. I'm kind of preoccupied."

Russ flopped in the recliner and turned on the television. He flipped through the channels until he found a weather report for the Oregon coast.

"Just what I was afraid of," he said to himself. The weather at the Coast was supposed to be one of those rare perfect "beach days." He knew he should have asked Laura if he could join her instead of acting like he cared more about a stupid game. The beach would be alive with single guys tomorrow, and, if he couldn't reach her, he wouldn't be among them.

He decided to let it ride until tomorrow morning, and show up at her place at 9 a.m. to see if he could join her for a day at the beach. Just because he hadn't thought fast enough earlier didn't mean he couldn't correct the situation. If their relationship was ever going to move forward, he was going to have to find some time to be alone with her. He loved Aunt Esther and was fond of Ernie, but you couldn't make a move with two elderly observers.

"Anyway, I can't," he said to Hammer.

RUSS KNEW HE WAS taking a chance by just showing up on Laura's front porch the next morning, but it was worth a shot. He had risen early, driven down to a yuppie deli that opened at 7 a.m., and paid an outlandish price for a picnic lunch for two that came ready-packed. He could see various cheeses, fruit, bread sticks, and a bottle of wine tucked in under a small red and white checked cloth.

He'd bungled this whole thing, he thought. If he'd asked Laura yesterday, she probably would have offered to pack the lunch.

He drove at break-neck speed back to her driveway. The truck was still there and her front door was hanging open.

He looked through the open doorway. "Am I too late to go to the beach with you?"

"Depends on who you are," she called back from upstairs where she was stuffing a sweatshirt and change of clothes in a beach bag.

"I'm the guy who should have jumped at the chance yesterday," he said.

"Oh, that guy," she said as she came downstairs. "Change of heart?"

"No," he said. "I just didn't think fast enough yesterday. Would you like company?"

"Do you promise to drive more slowly than when you took me to the emergency room?"

"That depends on whether you're going to get hit by a dump truck between here and the driveway," he answered.

"Funny. Very funny," she said. Then she realized he was still waiting for an answer. "I'd love to have company." She glanced at the lunch basket. "Particularly company who can pack a fancy lunch."

"Great."

"I hope you have a change of clothes along," she said.

"Just what do you have planned?" he asked.

"Probably not what you're thinking," she said. "I've never gone for a walk along the breach that I didn't get caught by a wave."

"Oh," he said, obviously disappointed.

There were probably only a dozen days a summer that could be declared "perfect weather" at the Oregon coast. Laura had chosen one of the twelve. When they arrived at their favorite strip of sand, the bright sun glistened on the water, and was cooled slightly offshore by a quiet breeze. Seagulls dipped in and out of the waves to select their food, and brightly colored kites flew above. Two surfers in wetsuits braved the waves, but otherwise the long stretch of beach where they spread their blanket belonged to Russ and Laura.

"Let's take that walk first and see if we can get you drenched," Russ suggested.

"Thanks a lot," she said, and took off running toward the waves, leaving him panting when he caught up with her.

He grabbed her hand and said, "Hey, a little consideration for an older man here." He didn't let go of her hand when they started jumping waves, as carefree as school children on an end-of-the-year field trip.

They walked farther south than they realized, and were left breathless when they finally turned around and walked back toward the blanket. They each had a pair of sandals dangling from their free hands and enjoyed the feel of the wet sand squishing between their toes. As they came around a cove, Russ slipped his hand around her waist and pulled her against him. "Do you need to take a rest?" he asked.

"That depends on what you have in mind," she said.

"This," he said. He dropped his sandals, put both arms around her and kissed her soundly.

"Oh, that," she said. "I thought you were thinking this." She wrapped her left hand around his neck and used the other to rub his bare back as she returned the kiss. The kiss lengthened until they heard the unmistakable voices of small children approaching the cove. They separated and walked on down to the blanket which now looked very inviting to Russ.

"Do you suppose our next job could be in a beach town?" Laura asked. "I could get used to spending my break times and weekends at the beach."

"I could get used to doing *this*, too," he said as he finished rubbing some suntan lotion onto her shoulders.

They stretched out on their stomachs on the blanket, side by side. Russ reached over and put his arm around her waist and pulled her in closer. When she had stripped down, he'd been surprised to see the bikini. To him, she looked like a *Sports Illustrated* swimsuit edition model in the two strips of black fabric.

"You do know, don't you," she said, "that you'll ruin my tan line with your arm there."

"Tough," he said and pulled her closer. Exhausted from a long work week, their extended walk down the beach, and now the warmth of the sun, they both drifted off to sleep.

By the time Laura woke up, the sun was lower in the sky and the air had cooled. Russ was awake and pretended to look around for the lunch basket. When he didn't see it, he asked Laura if she had moved it while he slept.

"You didn't eat it while I was asleep, did you?" she asked.

"No. Of course not. I know I brought it down here when we came from the truck. Did you notice it when we got back from our walk?" he asked.

"I don't remember."

"Damn," he said. "As I see it, we have two choices. I tackle one of those seagulls and hijack his lunch, or we gather up our things here and stop in town for a seafood dinner."

"Is there a half-way decent place?" she asked.

"Only the one where I made reservations," he said. "By the way, the picnic box is in the shade in the cab of the truck," he confessed. "I decided I'd rather sit at a window table with you and watch the lights play across the waves crashing outside."

"When did you decide all this?" she asked.

"Right after I saw you in that black swimsuit," he said honestly. "I knew I wanted to be with you more than three or four hours."

"Me too," she said.

They put their fresh clothes on over the swimsuits and headed back to the truck and up the coast a mile or two where there was a restaurant on a bluff overlooking the ocean.

"We'd like a private table for two," he said when they entered. "Something secluded, if you have it," he added as he handed the man a twenty dollar bill.

"Sure you didn't have this planned ahead?" Laura asked.

"No," he insisted. "It came to me when I was watching you sleep. You're a very sexy sleeper."

WHEN THEY DROVE back to Portland, both of them became quiet. Russ wondered if Laura was thinking the same thing he was. Russ' main house at Graham Construction was within view of Esther's quarters. While they were adults and could do as they pleased, they certainly didn't want their behavior to create any tension within the work team.

"You hungry?" Laura asked as if she could read his mind.

"Always."

"Instead of dropping me off, why don't you come in and we'll have that wine in front of the fireplace at my house?"

"Perfect."

Louise was discreet, and never mentioned what time Russ left.

IT WAS TIME SOMEONE took charge and found out what was going on out at the Street of Dreams, Esther thought. The police seemed eager to take reports each time something criminal occurred, but Esther saw no indication of them trying to find the "perp," or, for that matter, solve the case of Sal Martinelli's murder. The vandalism was costing Graham Construction money. The unsolved Martinelli case was costing them sleep.

Late Friday night, Esther looked around to make sure there were no lights on in Russ' quarters at Graham Construction, and then quietly moved downstairs and outside to load her supplies into the back of her aging Honda Element. The engine wasn't as quiet as it was when her mechanical steed rolled out of the showroom, but the vehicle still served her well.

She debated how to hide the bright orange and gray rig at the Dreams site, then packed a camouflage blanket with her other supplies. A flashlight, hearty snacks, a baseball bat, her mystery novel, mace . . . She planned to pull to the far end of the driveway and cover the rear of the car with the Army Surplus blanket. She'd leave her car keys in the Element in case she had to make a quick getaway during the night.

She left her apartment and drove to the Italianate house with no complications. Now she placed her house key in the back door lock, and quietly entered the house. She fumbled through the kitchen in the dark until she reached her destination. There was no point in blowing her cover now by turning on a light. Who knew if Wart was on the job tonight?

"So far, so fab," she thought as she arranged a down comforter nest for herself in the pantry. She balanced her Derrick Jeter autographed baseball bat next to the door framing and put the flashlight and her trusty spray can of mace on the floor next to the hand grip on the bat. She settled in and sat for five minutes before ripping off the top on the six-pack—of miniature powdered sugar donuts.

She checked her glow-in-the-dark watch for the third time since she had arrived. She had been in her pantry hideout for seventeen minutes. She thought belatedly that she should have added a radio to her supplies for entertainment and some potato chips to her overnight rations. At this rate, the thermos of coffee and bag of Cheetos would be gone in no time.

As one-woman stakeouts went, this one was pretty comfortable. And, if she discovered someone entering the house, she was prepared to "take him down" and call the police on her new cell phone.

Esther was late joining the Technology Age, but the sales clerk at the AT&T counter had been extremely patient as he explained the features on the phone to her last week. He even programmed her flip phone to call 911 with the press of a single number. She'd had the phone for over two weeks now, but hadn't told Russ and Laura yet. She wanted to be more at ease with the device before she used it in public.

Somewhere among all her snack items was the post-it note where the clerk had written the number to push for 911. Unfortunately, she couldn't find the small yellow piece of paper or the new phone anywhere among the jumble of snacks. Then, she remembered where she'd last seen the cell phone. She had left it attached to the charger, resting on the side counter in her small kitchen at home.

Esther swung the shuttered door to the pantry shut and read by the light of the flashlight for forty-five minutes to an hour before she dozed off. She awoke to the sound of a hammer hitting nails and driving them each forcefully into wood.

She managed to untangle herself from the comforter and rose to her feet in the cramped quarters to open the swinging pantry door. The door wouldn't budge. Someone was holding a piece of plywood tight against the door and nailing it to the door frame. It was crude carpentry, but it prevented her from opening the door. Whoever wielded the hammer knew what he was doing.

She slumped into the corner of the pantry and forced herself to stay quiet. She sized up the situation and calmed herself when she realized that she would have fresh air coming in through two knot holes in the low-grade plywood. Unless someone set fire to the place. She quickly discarded the thought. Whoever wielded that hammer could have simply hit her on the head with it if he'd wanted her dead.

Some detective she'd turned out to be, she thought. She could tell by the sound of the shoes leaving the kitchen that her captor had worn tennis shoes, but there was no way to tell if they were Nikes or Adidas. Any self-respecting Oregon thug would have gone for the first.

She sighed and reached for the thermos of coffee. It would be a long weekend.

WARD SIMMONS WAS on the job this Friday night, but he only planned to make the rounds once before heading home. He thought he was entitled to a break, too, as the weekend approached. He wouldn't have done that much, but he didn't know for sure if some of the new homes already had security cameras in place. So much the better for him if they did, he thought. He wanted to be able to prove to his employers that he was doing his job. At least for twenty minutes each night. The rest of the night he sacked out at the social center near the stocked refrigerator.

He was surprised to find that there was a vehicle parked at the Graham Construction site. He also thought he heard noise coming from inside the house. Or, maybe his imagination was in overdrive.

There was no choice. He was going to have to enter the house. Tomorrow morning he'd demand that he be allowed to carry a gun on this job. For now, he had the folding knife in the sheath on his belt.

He backed off the porch to gather his courage. When he looked up he saw the damage to the back siding on the house. Someone had splashed what looked like a five-gallon can's worth of blood red paint against the back of the house.

Ward breathed a little easier now that he was convinced that it was kids who were the culprits. It beat dealing with someone who was intent on burning down the old Italianate place or lying in wait to attack the night watchman.

He wasn't taking any chances, though. He entered the back door as quietly as he could, using the key that Graham Construction had begrudgingly supplied for him. After helping himself to a beer from the refrigerator, he heard the noise again. He still couldn't identify the sound, but as he got closer to the dining room, he thought he heard snoring. He returned to the kitchen and discovered the muted sounds were coming from the pantry.

The damned kids thought he was running a free motel. He'd show them.

He turned on his heavy duty flashlight and walked through the house. Graham had left the place all swept and tidy for the weekend but there had to be a hammer somewhere.

He glanced around and saw a full piece of plywood leaning against the other end of the kitchen counter. It was the perfect size. The hammer he needed had been in plain site on the counter all along. With four direct hits from the hammer, he nailed the plywood across the pantry door.

"Damn kids think they're so smart," he said later as he yanked the blanket off the car outside. Then he started to worry. "What if the kids get loose during the night and drive to the police station?" he wondered.

With the influence of a third beer, he developed a plan. He'd bet the kids had left the keys in the car. If the keys were there, he'd drive it down the winding road.

Bingo. The keys were in the ignition. He started the car, drove less than half a mile and backed it into a dirt side road that angled off the main paved one. He drove about fifty feet and then came to a stop. In case there was an honor student in the group who figured out that the car might be hidden down the road, he took extra measures so the kids couldn't get to the police.

He pulled his knife out and punched the front left tire. The whoosh of the air escaping the tire was exhilarating. He punched another. When he walked back up to the Street of Dreams, all four tires on Esther's car were flat.

Even if the punks did find the car in the dark, they wouldn't be going anywhere, Simmons thought.

WHEN ESTHER WASN'T home Sunday morning and there was no note on her kitchen counter saying where she had gone, Laura panicked, and began calling hospital emergency rooms.

"No, Esther Graham had not been admitted," she heard on the first call. The message was the same from every hospital in the area.

What if Aunt Esther hadn't returned safely from her snack run Friday night? What if she never got to the spa on Saturday? Laura kicked herself for not checking on Esther before taking her own daytrip to the beach on Saturday. It would have taken thirty seconds to drive past and see if Essie's distinctive car was parked at Graham Construction.

Russ offered to drive out to the Dreams site in case Aunt Esther had gotten confused and showed up to work early on a weekend morning. He hadn't seen any signs of dementia, but Esther was, after all, getting older.

Before he could back out of the driveway, his cell phone sounded. It was the police calling to report that they had found Esther's car on a dirt road near the construction sites. This didn't look good.

WARD PULLED UP in front of the Italianate house behind Russ. He greeted him warmly and tried to impress Russ with how alert he was in noticing anyone approaching the property on a weekend when the crews were gone.

"Is there trouble out here?" he asked, producing his key to the place. "You wait outside," he told Russ authoritatively. "I'm the watchman here."

Russ started to protest, but decided to humor the man. He'd be two steps behind him. They both heard the mumbled sounds as they entered.

"Who's in there?" Ward called out to impress Russ with his bravery.

"It's Esther Graham, you idiot," came the answer. "Get me out of here."

"Where are you?" he asked innocently.

"In the pantry. P-A-N-T-R-Y!"

"What are you doing in there?" Ward asked.

"Listen carefully," Esther said between clenched teeth. "Remove the sheet of plywood."

"How?"

"There's a crowbar on the side porch," she said, enunciating each word. "Bring it into the house. Use it on the door," she spit out. "When the door is free, hand the crow bar to me," she continued. "I'm going to use it to beat you silly."

"There's no need to be nasty," he said.

Russ had sized up the situation more quickly than Ward and was already returning to the kitchen with the tool. He handed the crow bar to Ward and stepped back.

Russ had to give Ward credit. Once he had the tool in hand, he freed Esther quickly and then dialed 911 (because he hadn't left his new cell phone on the charger) and asked for police assistance. The officers on routine patrol in the area arrived within five minutes.

They repeated the details surrounding the discovery of Esther's car, and added that they'd been able to pick up some good shoe prints in the area around the car. Ward shuffled his own feet awkwardly. (Keds, Esther noted.)

"Is there something we need to know here, Mr. Simmons?" the first cop asked.

"Not at all," he responded. "I checked the perimeter of this house in the early morning hours, but didn't find anything amiss."

"What brought you to this site in particular?" the officer asked.

"I check all the places. I'm extra diligent on the weekends," he said. "I want these folks to return Monday mornings to a safe work environment."

"Hmmmm," the officer said. "Would you mind if I took a closer look at your left shoe?"

Ward looked confused.

"The one with red paint on it," the officer responded. "The spilled paint outside has been dry for several hours, but there are red shoe prints here by the pantry door."

"Oops!" Ward said quietly. He hesitated a minute, and took a deep breath while he looked at his paint spattered shoes. "I thought it was kids, officer, and I was going to teach them a lesson," he said.

"You're going to need more than 'oops' here, Buster," Esther answered.

"How 'bout I pay the insurance deductible on the car for you?"

"What's wrong with my car?" she asked.

"The tires kind of went flat last night," he confessed.

"How about you forget that first offer and up-step those wheels to sixteen inchers with new rims and chromies."

Chromies? Now there was a word the cop hadn't heard in years, but he stayed out of the discussion. The civil part of this case was strictly between the Graham woman and Simmons. He still had to figure out if false imprisonment charges would stand up in court. He supposed he could lessen the charge against Edward Simmons to "stupidity."

The cops wrote a brief report, took down information from the three present, and gave them each a business card with a case number written on it for future reference. Esther and Russ knew the drill.

"Do you have any other questions before we go back on patrol?"

Russ was quiet, still recovering from the adrenaline rush he'd experienced when he realized that Esther had been trapped in the house two nights. Ward Simmons was trying to fade into the background, wondering how long it would be before he was fired, and if it would be by phone or in person Monday morning.

"Could you please witness that I advised Mr. Simmons that I expect restitution as I described earlier by no later than Wednesday?" Esther asked the officer.

"Otherwise, I might have to call you gentlemen back to hear him explain why he helped himself to the beer in our refrigerator late last night."

The officers made no comment, but sent Ward on his way while Russ contacted Laura to assure her Esther was safe. Laura still couldn't shake the guilt over not having dialed Esther's number Friday night to make sure that Esther had returned safely from the alleged milkshake run. What was nagging at Russ was that, if Esther's timing had been slightly different, she could have walked right into a deranged person armed with a can of blood red paint and who knew what else.

"You do know you could have been killed?" Russ asked Esther.

"By Wimpy Wart?" Esther answered. "The ass who assaulted my car? Who would slash all four tires? It only takes one to cripple a car."

"Don't change the subject," Russ said firmly. "What if no one had found you until Monday morning?"

"I'd have lost a little weight?"

"You're not taking this threat very seriously," Russ said, mimicking the cops' past admonitions to Laura.

"That reminds me," Esther said. "Did I remember to tell you I've lost seventeen pounds?"

"How did that happen?" Russ asked to humor her.

"It's a long story, but I'll make it short," she said. "I don't think my weight is any of the State of Oregon's damn business. So each time I renew my drivers' license, I take off another five to seven pounds when I fill out the form. In another five years I'll be downright svelte."

Russ suggested they pick up Laura and the three of them go to breakfast at the local Denny's and then he'd return to the building site to see if additional damage had occurred during the night. The police had the report on the painted graffiti, but Russ was more concerned about making sure the grounds were safe for his work crew to return on Monday.

"What was written on the house?" Laura asked during breakfast.

"There's a giant splash of red paint. There's no way we could miss it," Russ said. "Around the corner in huge letters, it says 'tear down,' but whoever it was misspelled 'tear.'"

"That lets out Francesca," Esther noted. "Or she thought there wasn't enough room to write 'demolish this abomination, *s'il vous plaît.*'"

THE POLICE followed up Monday morning, reviewing video from the three homes where builders had already installed exterior home security cameras. There were three sections of footage that, while of interest, didn't provide any help in solving the mysteries on the Street of Dreams. They elected not to share the film with the builders and decorators. Those folks wouldn't miss seeing deer eating Helen Parker's petunias, Edward Simmons urinating against the side of the social center, or Francesca Childers using the neighbors hose after hours to keep her own water bill low.

"Light color paints dry lighter than they look when wet. Dark colors dry darker."

26

Graham Construction's goal was to return the grand Italianate home to its former splendor, both in structure and in furnishings.

"Within reason," Russ would add whenever he could get a word in between Laura and Esther's comments about the ideal way to "stage" the home for the open house.

That was one of the primary differences in the sales approach used in selling subdivision new construction and selling the new homes on the Street of Dreams. Every inch of the Dreams homes would be staged with rental and borrowed furniture. The decorator or designer at each site even selected dinnerware and silverware patterns to have displayed on the rented kitchen table. The Italianate home would be in competition with the others on the block and needed to have pizzazz to set it apart from the rest of the neighborhood.

Laura was several steps away from the staging process, though. She was still perplexed about three tiny rooms upstairs, only one of which had a window. It was a wonderful large window with a built-in upholstered bench that opened for storage, but it was in a room that couldn't have been more than seven by eight feet.

"Let's measure this room," Laura said to Esther who had taken to carrying a tape measure, an X-acto knife and extra blades with her at all times. The blades were perfect for trimming wallpaper along the crown moldings and baseboards.

"The room's smaller than we thought," Esther said. She put her tape measure back in her pocket. "Who has a six by seven room in a house this size?"

"I think this area was originally all one room that was later partitioned," Laura said.

"Did you see the names scribbled with red crayon in the back corner?" Esther asked. "I looked, but the list doesn't include 'Francesca.'"

"I'm glad you mentioned her. Let's stroll up the block and see if she can give us any history about this chopped up floor plan. I know these dividing walls aren't original."

Francesca Childers greeted them cordially but didn't seem eager to have company. She balanced a stemmed glass in her left hand as she showed them inside and asked if they would like to join her with a glass of wine. Laura turned her down and Esther mumbled "No thanks" as she inhaled sharply after Laura elbowed her.

"We wanted to ask you about the upstairs rooms on the west side of your family's former home." Laura thought mentioning Francesca's tie to the home might work in her favor in pulling out the information she wanted.

"Oh yes," Francesca said. She hesitated a moment, then added, "How can we help you?"

Esther assumed the "we" referred to Francesca and the glass of merlot in her hand, as no one else was present when they arrived.

"It looks like one large upstairs room, the one with remnants of pink wallpaper, was cut up into several smaller rooms at some point."

"Oh, that," Mrs. Childers said. "It was my room. Of course, I remember," she said. "Mother and Grandmother persuaded my father to partition the end of that large, lovely room for me. That gave me my own tiny tea room for my friends, a room for toys, and . . ."

She hesitated as though she couldn't remember what the third tiny space was there for in the past. "Oh, of course. My walk-in closet."

"There are some names written on the wall," Esther said.

Francesca had another sip of wine and then paused as if remembering her girlhood in the house might be painful.

"You found those, did you? Those were the girls who attended my Sweet Sixteen party," she recalled. "I knew I would have been in bad trouble if Mother had ever seen that defaced wall so my friends Catherine and Cecelia helped me pull the chiffonier into the little room to cover the names."

"Chiffonier?" Esther asked.

"A tall armoire or closet with a mirrored door on one side and drawers on the other," Francesca explained. The words were fine, but the tone said "how could you be so stupid?"

"Thank you for the help," Laura said ushering Esther, who still secretly wanted some wine, to the door. "We have to get back now."

"Yes," said Esther. "We need to move the *escritoire* into the grand foyer."

They were 100 feet up the block before Laura asked "What's an escritoire?"

"Unless my high school French teacher failed me, it's a secretary or writing desk," Esther said. "It's from the Latin *scriptorium*."

"You took both French and Latin in high school?" Laura asked.

"No. I took the Latin course in college to help with medical terminology. Unfortunately, an emergency room nurse never has a chance to plop her back side in a chair, let alone use the *escritoire*."

"The classes were worth it to see the look on Mrs. Childers' face." Laura said. "It sounds like Francesca was a spoiled brat as a child."

"Rich bitches start young." Esther said. "She sure didn't want to talk about the house."

"Maybe it was the wine."

"You think?"

They walked down the street.

"Did you buy that malarkey about her sixteenth birthday party?"

"I guess I didn't give it much thought," Laura answered. "Maybe they were really close friends."

"I was sixteen once, and my crowd and I were definitely beyond the age of writing our names on the wall with lipstick. Boys' names, maybe, but not our own."

Laura raised an eyebrow, but didn't respond.

"On second thought," Esther said, "It was probably her hit list when she didn't have a date yet for the Valentines' Day Dance."

ESTHER, RUSS, AND LAURA had gathered at the make-shift table in the kitchen of the project house to review timelines and expenses as the remodel neared completion. As Russ rose to return to work, he reached for the overflowing trash can to take it out to the dumpster.

"Don't take that trash can out," Laura cautioned. "There's something in it I need to show you."

Laura put a plastic bag around her hand and reached into the trash can.

"The plastic bag is to prevent fingerprints," she said. "I'm learning."

"I don't know if that works," Russ said. "Pfeifer could tell you." He regretted that last sentence as soon as it was out of his mouth. He respected Pfeifer, but he'd always seen him as competition for Laura's attention.

"It's a mannequin's hand," Laura said as she pulled out a flesh-colored form that looked like it should have been on a glass sales counter wearing several pieces of jewelry. "It was on the front porch this morning, and it was holding the note that's on the kitchen counter."

"Now you're telling us this?" Russ asked. "We've been here twenty minutes. When did you plan to mention it?"

"Did it freak you out?" Esther asked.

"Not really. I could tell it was a fake," Laura said. "Once you've seen the real thing, nothing else compares."

"Let's see the note." Russ said.

"There's not much to look at. It says BURN THIS HOUSE."

"Very succinct," Russ said. "Do you recognize the handwriting?"

"No. One thing's for sure, though," she said. "The writer would have a hard time hitting a word count for a full length book."

"There you go again being flip about what could be very serious," Russ said. "Call Pfeifer."

"Not."

"There's an open, on-going investigation, Laura. You need to contact the guy."

"I'll talk to him next time he stops by," she said. "If I keep calling the police bureau, Esther's front desk guy is going to think I'm hitting on Pfeif."

"Are you?" he asked.

"Go pound some nails."

"ME AGAIN," Charmaigne called out as she peeked in the front door, looking for Laura.

Laura groaned, but greeted the designer with a friendly wave and a hello from the stairs where she was using steel wool to take the rough edges off the banister.

"Gary suggested I come calling and see how you all are doing since the vandalism and all," she said.

"I'll bet he did," Laura thought. She had to admire the man for spending eight hours a day with Charmaigne's constant chatter. Laura recalled that during the first two weeks they had all been on site, Charmaigne had come over to the Graham Construction project three different days and each time introduced herself, apparently having forgotten overnight that she had come "a-callin'" the day before.

"I'm not sure I'd have the patience to re-do an old place like this," Charmaigne said. "I can't imagine having to take off old cruddy finish and having to strip wallpaper and all the rest of the stuff I keep finding you doing. It must be hell on manicures."

"I could let Russ and the subs do all this, but I like being part of the whole re-make," Laura said. "I get some of my best decorating ideas while I'm doing grub labor. I can let my mind wander and see this place how it probably looked when it was first built and how it's going to look when it's completed this time around."

"Well I admire that. It's just so down and dirty. Did I tell you about the clean look and sleek fixtures I have planned for the baths next door? Of course we have a humungous tub in that master bath. I hope a couple buys the place because it's big enough for two."

Laura nodded.

"'Two' reminds me. Have you heard from that builder of yours?"

Laura didn't tell her that Russ was back, but let the woman prattle on. Charmaigne's thoughts caromed back and forth like the balls on a pool table following the break.

"Did I tell you I saw the homeless guy that everyone reports they've seen around here? He reminded me of someone from my past life, but, of course, I couldn't remember who. Do you believe in coincidences? I can't believe it's just coincidence that we wound up working next door to each other."

"How do you think it happened?" Laura asked out of curiosity.

"Karma," Charmaigne said simply. "Gotta go. I need to see the dining alcove at our place in late afternoon light. Like when someone would be setting the table. Say at 4:47 in the afternoon. I always like to have the table set well in advance. Bye for now."

And, she was off.

"Way off," Laura thought.

RUSS HAD INSPECTED the work by the electrical and plumbing contractors immediately upon his return. It met with his satisfaction and he knew it would pass the inspections scheduled for the next week. Building codes were in place for a reason and he never wanted to be responsible for injury or unneeded expenditures by the new owners because of shoddy workmanship by those he hired.

He'd also been pleased with the tile work completed while he was away. He knew that Laura would select product well, but he had no idea of the craftsmanship that would be evident in Ernie's work.

"Hell, if I were house hunting, I'd buy this place for the tile work alone," Russ thought. It was both beautiful and practical. The entry screamed out for live plants and it wouldn't matter if the water dripped through to the flooring. He'd like to hang onto Ernest Gallo until the house was completely remodeled and maybe have him on call into the future. Pride in craftsmanship and good work ethic had been missing in most of the applicants who had interviewed with Graham Construction in the past few years.

When Ernie arrived, Russ gave the tile work a five-star review and asked Ernie if he would consider staying on for a while.

"I'd have to give it some thought," Ernie said. "I wouldn't want to hang around for 'make work' tasks. Do you have some jobs I could pick up hit and miss to take some of the load off your shoulders?"

"Absolutely. If the electrical and plumbing inspections sail through as I expect, we'll be able to start the installation and tile work in the bathrooms."

"A little early isn't it?" Ernie asked.

"You're right there," Russ said. "But when you work on a team where you're outnumbered by women, you make some concessions. It might be nice if Laura and Esther didn't have to troop back and forth to the so-called social center to use the restroom. They nixed the portable outhouses."

"Kinda soft on those two, aren't you?" Ernie asked.

"They've both got a way of getting under your skin."

"No argument there," Ernie said. He walked toward the bench in the corner to deposit his thermos and lunchbox. He'd given up the crock pot when the thermometer on the outside of the house passed ninety degrees.

"Not that it's any of my business," Ernie said, "but did you and Laura patch things up?"

"It's better, but we're still kind of running in place," Russ answered.

"My advice is to ease the conversation toward the future," Ernie said quietly. "Wait," he added. "I don't think I heard either of you ask for my advice. Cancel that."

"Does that work?" Russ asked.

"Did for me," he said, thinking of his late wife. "Either mope or make your move. That's my motto."

"OK," Russ said.

"OK, that's enough advice. Or, OK you'll try it?"

"I don't have any choice," Russ said. "Being in limbo like this is driving me crazy. I didn't think I'd ever feel this way about a woman."

"Tell her. Not me."

"Gotcha."

"There's something I'd been planning to ask you when you got yourself back here," Ernie said. He hesitated and Russ waited. "I don't suppose you'd object or anything like that if I invited that aunt of yours out to dinner some time."

"Ernie, my man, how well do you know my Aunt Essie?"

"Not all that well. That's why I thought we might spend some time away from here and get better acquainted."

"You have my blessing. Though you hardly need it," Russ said. "But I've got to warn you, Esther is not your normal, sedate senior citizen."

"Good. That's what I was hoping for," Ernie said and headed back to the job at hand. Notes of *Fly Me to the Moon* competed with the country music coming from a car stereo at one of the other work sites.

"Eliminate extra furniture pieces with built-in cabinets & shelves. No one can have too many drawers."

27

The thermometer read 101 degrees and Laura felt every one of those degrees. It was no surprise to her that heat rises, and she was sweltering. She was looking at the upstairs space that had been Francesca's childhood bedroom, trying to decide how to decorate the lovely room created when the partitions were removed.

Laura thought the small closet-sized spaces at the end of the room had looked like stalls in a barn. And, what little girl needed her own tea room?

She looked over the large re-created space again and decided that this room would be perfect as a bedroom for the young princesses of a modern couple. It was too much square footage for one child. And, with the sunlight coming in from the window that had been shut off in the former tea room, the space was now flooded with light. A happy room. Even on the rainiest Oregon day, she thought.

Laura wasn't used to designing "fluffy" rooms, but this space spoke to her and it said in no uncertain terms that it wanted to be soft, feminine and pretty.

Esther and Ernie were downstairs. She could hear them chatting and then heard Esther's footsteps on the stairs.

The whistled notes of *Stars Fell on Alabama* wafted up the stairs as Ernie worked. It surprised Laura. Lately he'd been back on *Fly Me to the Moon*. Esther stepped into the upstairs room and immediately began fanning herself with her hands.

"If you'd left one of those tiny closet-rooms up here, you could have had a sauna," she said.

"Nope. It's going to be a beautiful spacious room, decorated and furnished for two little girls to share."

"Pink?"

"No. I'm going with the softest mint green and cream. I can't take the thought of stripping all the faded old pink floral paper off and then turning the room pink again," Laura said.

"Agreed."

Laura and Russ had talked about a date to have all the wood floors in the house refinished. In this room she'd have one area covered by a soft floral rug—a rug with a design where little feet could jump from flower to flower—and leave one area where the hardwood was exposed for those same feet in small ballet shoes to practice dance routines.

Esther moved from one window to the next, circling the room and looking out toward the Portland hills.

"On a clear night those little girls will be able to see the stars out these windows. It'll be just like Wendy in Peter Pan, sitting on the window seat and watching for falling stars in the night sky."

ESTHER WAS TIRED. She decided to stay out in her roof garden and have a second cup of coffee with her breakfast. Laura had both Russ and Ernie at the site now so she definitely didn't need her there all hours of the day, Esther thought. It was so much easier to do her bookkeeping in her office at Graham Construction headquarters. Some warm days, Hammer stayed home and kept her company.

She hadn't slept much last night. She had started by worrying if Laura's choice of little girl pastel colors upstairs in the Dreams house would limit the number of possible buyers. Her brain moved from there to wondering if Laura would ever have children of her own. She hated to see Laura let her life slip by because she had been too busy to have children. Esther knew all about that.

Esther finished her second cup of coffee and thought she'd enjoy the morning air a few minutes more. She woke up two hours later and looked around. Hammer was asleep at her feet.

"Ah, retirement!" she said to the dog. She cleared the breakfast table and invited Hammer to go to the building site with her. It promised to be a cooler day, but, if she was wrong and the weather grew too warm, she could always bring him home early.

She hoped Ernie had packed cold Italian meatballs and mozzarella sandwiches today. That man could cook. And, he didn't mind sharing.

HAMMER GREETED RUSS like it had been weeks since they'd all been together. Russ had actually taken Hammer for a 5 a.m. walk before heading for the job site.

Laura waited until she and Esther were alone to ask why Esther looked so tired.

"Couldn't sleep last night," Esther said. "I started wondering what would happen if the potential buyers for this place didn't have little girls. Then my brain kept rolling."

"Not to worry."

"Now you tell me," Esther interrupted. "Where were you at 3 a.m. when I couldn't sleep?"

"The two other auxiliary bedrooms will be more gender neutral. I'm doing one in a crisp navy and white nautical look. The other one will be soft aqua, the same color you suggested earlier for Vivian's scarf."

"How is Vivian?" Esther asked.

"In recovery."

"You have so much fun working up these kid motif bedrooms. Do you ever want kids of your own?" Esther asked.

"I haven't given it much thought. Maybe someday. Right now I can't afford to even think about it."

"If people waited until they could afford kids, they'd never have any," Esther said.

"I'd also prefer to have a father for those kids who is going to stick around, not go gallivanting off to Mexico." She hesitated, then said, "I can sure pick 'em. That's why I was so ready to believe Russ was in Louisiana hitting the bars and strip clubs. I feel bad about that."

"Not all men are alike," Esther said.

"But, a lot of them are," Laura said. "I'd rather be alone for two lifetimes than end up with someone like Wart."

"I think Wart's married."

"No!" Laura exclaimed.

"Stranger things have happened."

THERE WERE A LOT of reasons originally why the Graham Construction partners were glad they had been selected this year to participate in the Street of Dreams project.

They may have gotten off to a rocky start with a dead body on the property, but they were trying to let the police worry about that while they concentrated on the project at hand.

Laura had already switched to lighter weight clothes earlier in the summer. Not the skimpy halter tops and deep slit skirts that Charmaine was wearing, but more practical cotton shirts and shorts. She couldn't remember a hotter summer. She also couldn't remember a summer that she hadn't said that.

The professional painters had been brought in to spray the ceilings, but she was now adding hand painted medallion patterns around the ceiling light fixtures. It was tedious and hot work. It also made her neck hurt to be looking up most of the day.

She thought of poor Vivian again. Such a senseless act.

And, then, as always, her thoughts drifted to Russ. He'd done his best to restore Vivian. Laura didn't think she had ever met a man as patient as Russ. She thought about him every day. His tall, muscular frame and the dark wavy hair that curled when he waited too long between haircuts . . . His blue eyes that gave away his amusement before the smile parted his lips. . . If he were a surgeon instead of a contractor, women who didn't look as fine as Vivian would be lining up at his office for chin lifts.

That's why Laura hadn't been surprised to learn that Charmaigne had apparently made a play for Russ right under Laura's nose. Charmaigne had definitely crossed the line with that move.

"There are countless methods for removing old wallpaper, but my favorite is the tried and true one of hiring someone else to do it."

28

Laura hadn't said anything to Russ or Esther, but, some mornings when she arrived at the Dreams site early, she had the eerie feeling that someone had been inside the place overnight. One morning she had found some scrap lumber stacked beneath the side window opening. Nothing seemed amiss inside, but it worried her.

Another day, when she arrived before the crew, she had seen Simmons (who had miraculously escaped with only a letter of reprimand after his night watchman fiasco!) coming around from the back of the house as she arrived.

"Everything's in order," he had called out to her.

"As if he would know," Laura thought. "The man doesn't know a piece of lumber from a foundation block."

She was afraid he was going to stop and chat so she walked directly to the front door and put her key in the lock. She called over her shoulder, wishing him a good day in her sweetest fake voice, entered, and quickly locked the door. She didn't trust the guy. Did he really spend his night watchman hours waiting for things to go bump in the night? Or, did he return to the site a few minutes before the work crews every morning?

She was glad Russ had persuaded Ernie to stay on the job. She felt safer when Ernie was already at work when she arrived.

"Besides, I'd miss those stars falling on Alabama," she told Louise.

Laura often debriefed the workday by talking to the cat. Louise didn't respond when Laura told him about Esther's experience locked in the closet by Ward Simmons, but she suspected the cat would concur with her opinion of the man.

Louise was a perceptive one and would attack without warning if she thought anyone needed to be put in their place. She lived by the popular cat philosophy of "scratch their eyes out first and ask questions later." Simmons wouldn't stand a chance.

ON WEDNESDAY, Esther mentioned that she was missing something she'd left at the Street of Dreams house when she'd stopped by at the end of the work day Tuesday. She remembered that everyone else was closing down for the day by the time she had arrived.

She had waved some invoices under Russ' nose for signatures and decided not to stick around long, she explained.

"You didn't leave something valuable here, did you?" Russ asked.

"That depends," she said. "I had a fresh-baked apple pie with me that wasn't quite cool enough to cut. Rather than cart it back home when I saw that you guys were winding up a little early, I put it under a cardboard box on the counter over there."

"The box that's on the floor?" Laura asked.

"It looks like the same one," Esther answered. "I'm not getting senile, am I? I know I put it here."

"Raccoons?" Ernie asked.

"Raccoons, yourself," Esther said. "They'd have eaten it all right, but they'd have left a mess."

Esther dropped the subject, but the others bemoaned the missing apple pie when break time came.

Esther showed up at the work site again on Thursday afternoon. This time she carried a batch of chocolate chip cookies on a covered metal plate.

"Help yourselves," she said, "but leave at least half a dozen on the plate."

Ernie didn't have to be invited twice and Russ was right behind him. Esther knew that Laura was working in her office at Graham Construction sorting through wheels of drapery material samples.

"These are great, Aunt Essie," Russ said, "but what's the occasion?"

"The Seventh of August."

He waited, chewing quietly. He knew more was coming.

"August is the only month without an official holiday," Esther said. "So I chose today to be one."

"And, what does one do *traditionally* to celebrate The Seventh of August? In addition to eating cookies, that is. Is it a joyous holiday or a patriotic one?"

"It's a vigilant holiday," Esther said.

She explained that she still hadn't forgiven whoever had taken her apple pie. She had carefully arranged the cookies on the plate, and she planned to catch the sweet-toothed thief tonight.

"You guys have your fill. Then you can scoot on home. I'll lock up."

Esther saw them out the door. Then, she turned to the plate containing the remaining cookies. Before placing the cardboard box over it, she reached in her pocket, the pocket where she carried her X-acto knife, and pulled out a small tube of SuperGlu. She opened the tube and, with the skill and care of a well-schooled registered nurse applying salve, she drew a beaded glue line around the entire outside edge of the plate. She pulled some toothpicks from the other pocket and used them to balance a pan lid above the platter.

Nights were already turning cool and she suspected the glue would stay liquid until it came in contact with something else. Like a cookie-snatching hand. She wished she could be here when the thief realized he had something on his hands and reached in his pocket for a handkerchief. Esther believed in swift justice.

She'd have a lot of explaining to do if no one entered during the night and either Russ or Ernie got there and reached for a snack first thing in the morning.

She'd jump that hurdle when and if she came to it.

"ESTHER, IS THAT YOU?" Russ said into his cell phone.

"If this is the number you called, it is," she answered.

"I need to talk to you about your chocolate chip cookie recipe," he said.

Darn! She'd forgotten. She should have been out at the site before the others got there.

"You're not attached to those cookies, are you?" she asked cautiously.

"I love 'em, but that's not why I called," he said. "While I was dialing you, I asked Ernie to call the EMT's for a non-life-threatening incident out here."

"Ernie's OK, then?" Esther asked.

"He's fine," Russ answered, "but Ward Simmons has managed to attach himself to the new kitchen faucet and the cookie plate with his left hand," Russ said. "His right hand is attached to the lid."

Esther didn't speak.

"Esther, I know you did this. Do you have anything to say to Mr. Simmons?"

"They could use a good cymbal player in the city band?" she suggested.

245

Russ groaned.

Esther tried again.   "That man's sure stuck on himself?"

Simmons yelled and Russ disconnected from the call with Aunt Esther. Ernie was standing in the doorway silently watching all the commotion.

"Was it Esther?" Ernie asked.

"I warned you," Russ said.

"If you'll excuse me," Ernie said, "I'm going to call that woman this minute and ask her out. Did you reach her at the business number?"

The EMTs arrived and freed Ward Simmons. He and Russ negotiated a friendly agreement that Graham Construction would not press charges for theft and Ward Simmons would not file a charge of assault and battery, thus averting what could have been a very sticky legal situation.

Russ was sure he heard the emergency crew chuckling as they walked back to their rig.

LOUD YELLING WAS coming from Gary and Charmaigne's building site at 10 a.m. on a Tuesday, and Laura started out the door to see if there was a problem over there.

"Not so fast," Esther said.

"With everything that's happened, I think I ought I to make sure she's all right."

Esther put a hand on Laura's arm to stop her mid step.

"I think she can hold her own," Esther said. "I saw Francesca Childers go in the side door over there about ten minutes ago."

"And, all that screeching is the two of them?"

"Mostly Francesca, I suspect," Esther said.

"I'd avoid an argument with that woman at all costs," Laura said. "Mrs. Childers has a mind like a steel trap and Charmaigne . . ."

". . . has a mind like a maze," Esther finished.

"That doesn't seem to deter the subcontractors on the other sites from coming and going at Charmaigne and Gary's place."

"She shows well," Esther said. "Until she opens her mouth."

The yelling continued for another few minutes. Laura was surprised there wasn't hair pulling and door slamming to go with it. She remembered belatedly that there weren't any doors hung over there yet.

"Small favors," she said to herself.

Jamen Childers arrived at the site five minutes later and escorted his mother across the roughed in front porch. Laura couldn't hear the complete conversation, but did hear Francesca dismiss the episode as "artistic differences, dear" as Jamen walked her up the block.

"Ignore the manufacturers' names of tints on paint sample strips. You're selecting a color, not naming a child."

29

Russ had done his best to repair the garden art. He called a concrete contractor and the two were able to use steel posts and cement to reassemble the statue. They weren't artists like Vivian's creator, but the repair job was barely noticeable to those who hadn't seen Vivian in two pieces. Nurse Esther contributed a neck brace of the type worn after whiplash injuries and Vivian was faithful about wearing it for the first two weeks after her surgery.

The shade garden plants were filling in nicely. The Graham Construction crew members were running ahead of schedule for the first time, and would definitely be ready to show the house on the opening weekend.

Laura, Esther and Russ had taken a late afternoon break and were sitting with Vivian who had been cleared by Esther to remove her neck brace. Three of the four of them were drinking mint-flavored iced tea Esther brought and were enjoying the late afternoon breeze.

The quiet was shattered by the sound of approaching sirens.

All the builders and their crews moved to the curbside in front of the houses, and peered up the block, waiting to see at which site the police cars would stop. Laura had seen four cars go past and could still hear what might be an ambulance siren wailing its way up the hill.

The first car stopped in front of Francesca and Jamen Childers' house. All the building teams on the street hung back, waiting to see what would develop. There were enough uniforms present to help, but it seemed like there should be something neighboring crews could do other than crane their necks and gawk.

The officers were there for over an hour before anyone came out of the home. Helen Parker, who was working with her husband on the house across the street, finally walked across the pavement, peeked in the front door and asked the nearest officer if she could be of comfort to either of the residents.

He politely, but firmly told her "a resident says 'absolutely not.' Those are the resident's words, not mine," he added. "But, please tell the neighbors we appreciate the thought. It'll probably be a few hours yet before we can release the name of the deceased."

Mrs. Parker stepped back off the porch. It hadn't occurred to her or any of the others that there might have been a fatality. When the ambulance had left soon after arriving, they had all assumed something much less dire.

The word of Jamen's death spread quietly and respectfully the next morning. The rumor was that the soft-spoken Jamen Childers had taken his own life. The news account that morning said he had been found by his mother who gave the police a note she found at the scene.

Laura wondered why it had been necessary to release the contents of such a personal note to the news reporters. It stated simply "I can't live with the secret. J."

"Is there no limit to the public's right to know?" Laura asked herself

WHEN LAURA ARRIVED at the Street of Dreams site at the end of the week, she found Charmaigne sitting on the front steps, holding two Starbucks cups of coffee. She offered one to Laura and sipped the other slowly. "They're both black," she said.

"This'll help me wake up," Laura said.

"I was awake all night crying over poor Jamen. I can't believe he's gone," Charmaigne said. "It's going to take all the courage I have to get through today."

"I don't think we're in personal danger," Laura said, trying to calm the woman.

"Oh, it's not just Jamen's death," the woman said. "I'm in a battle of wits."

Laura suspected Charmaigne's problem was probably as shallow as selecting a color of blush or deciding whether to wear her hair down or in a chignon for her next TV spot. Charmaigne made marshmallows look deep.

"How well do you know Detective Pfeifer?" she asked.

"Fairly well," Laura said slowly. "Why?"

"I may need to talk to him."

"Him specifically or just a detective?"

"I'm scared to death of your Detective Roberts," Charmaigne confided. "I thought maybe you could help me tell Detective Pfeifer something that is kind of important."

"How 'kind of important?'" Laura asked.

"The kind of important that makes me worry about how I'll look in horizontal stripes or a tacky orange jump suit."

"Let's go inside," Laura said more kindly. "I think you need to tell me what's going on before I call the cops out here again."

They sat down on the built-in window seat in the future library.

"Go!" Laura demanded.

"It's not that easy," Charmaigne said. "Before he died, Jamen told me I had to clear this up and that's what I'm going to do." She hesitated, before asking, "What is the penalty for filing a false police report?"

"How false?"

"Like pretty colossal."

Laura sipped her coffee and waited.

"You remember when you found me on your back porch?" Charmaigne asked.

"Of course."

"Nobody beat me up," she said. "There. I've said it!" she added. "I wasn't attacked or assaulted or anything like that."

"This isn't good," Laura said. "You filed a false police report?"

"And, I threatened my builder Gary. He promised not to tell that I was arguing with him and I tripped over a sawhorse he had placed at the top of the unfinished stairs so no one would get hurt."

"I need more," Laura said.

"The sawhorse had a red caution sign on it."

"More about the accident," Laura said.

"I was wearing fairly new boots with a stacked heel that Gary had warned me about before. I was spinning and twirling my skirt to show a little leg like they taught me to do on the TV spot," Charmaigne explained. "There was this loud sound up by the chimney. I thought it was gunfire and I lost my footing while I was trying to take cover."

"Have you ever heard a Northern Flicker," Laura asked.

"A northern what-er?"

"Never mind," Laura said. "Tell me more about the threat,"

"To Gary?" Charmaigne asked.

"Unless you've threatened anyone else lately."

"I told him I'd lie and report him for cutting corners on the electrical work after the inspector OK'd it if Gary ever told anyone what really happened," Charmaigne said. "Gary tried to stop the bleeding on my head. When that didn't work, he carried me through the backyards and put me on your porch. Gary is really strong," she added. "If you hadn't found me right away, he was supposed to come to the back door and 'discover' me there."

"I'm afraid to ask, but *why?*"

"I'm an OMG-TV star. I can't be portrayed as a klutz," she said. "I tripped and knocked over the sawhorse and fell down the stairs," she added. "Leak a story like that and my career will be down the toilet in a flash."

"Or a flush," Laura said.

"This is serious. This is my life!"

"Right," Laura said. "Let me jump ahead a step. You misreported this to the police and your insurance company?"

Charmaigne nodded.

"And, you let the police think everyone and anyone on the Street of Dreams project was a suspect," she said.

"I'm afraid so."

"And, as if that weren't enough," Laura said, "the police pointed the finger at Russ because he'd left after your accident and Mr. Martinelli's concrete experience?"

"Yes, again, I guess."

"So why come clean now?"

"Because I was stupid then. And now I'm scared."

"You should be," Laura said. "I appreciate the coffee, but what do you want me to do about all this?"

"Go to the Police Bureau with me?"

"Charmaigne, I think you need a lawyer, not a home decorator."

INSTANT REPLAY. Charmaigne was back sitting on the front porch of the Italianate house three mornings later with two recyclable cardboard cups filled with coffee. This time she had ordered the drinks with caramel flavoring, an extra shot of espresso and whipped cream with dark chocolate shavings on the top.

"You're back," Laura said. Stupid remark, she knew, but she needed the coffee and it was probably worth hearing about Charmaigne's woes again. The morning was cool and misty, and a warm drink would take the chill off.

"I did what you said," Charmaigne said.

"I didn't tell you what to do."

"You didn't, but the lawyer you told me to hire did."

Charmaigne repeated what she had learned from her attorney. In Oregon, knowingly filing a false police report is a Class C misdemeanor, carrying a penalty of fines up to $1250 and imprisonment up to 30 days.

"Oh, my Gawd," Laura said, choking on her coffee.

"It gets worse," Charmaigne said. "Providing false information to a police officer is a Class A misdemeanor which could mean a fine up to $6,250 and up to a year in a cell."

"What are you going to do?"

"I already did it," Charmaigne said. "My lawyer put together a plea bargain. I'm paying the larger fine and I agreed to go public with what really happened."

She threw her arms around Laura in an exaggerated hug. "And, you did it all for me," she said. "Maybe we could be friends for real now. I'd even let you call me Char."

"I'm proud of you," Laura said.

"Don't be proud yet," Char said. "I've just returned from talking to the owners at OMG-TV where I've negotiated to do several short spots on safety on the job site."

"And?"

"That should bring in a shitload of cash—about ten times the fine if I figured it out right." Char licked the whipped cream off her upper lip.

Laura was too stunned to speak.

"**I HAD A CALL** from Detective Roberts," Russ said. "I don't know what you did, Laura, but thank you."

"I didn't do anything."

"He said you were instrumental in removing a false police report from their files and I'm in the clear. On *everything* they've been investigating out at the Dreams."

"You're welcome," she said. She could have said more, but that was Char's job.

"Did I ever thank you, Laura, for managing this whole project while I was gone?" Russ asked.

"We're a team. You don't have to thank me."

"Well, I appreciate it," he said.

"I keep wondering who will move into this place. Sometimes I look at it as a wonderful, spacious, historic house. Other times, I'm sure we're going to be trying to sell this Italianate monstrosity for the next three years."

"It'll be somebody's dream house," he said. Ernie's advice rang in his ears.

"Just for fun," Russ said, "what would you want in a dream house?"

"I've never given it much thought," she answered.

"Say you and I were going to build our dream house," he started.

She didn't miss the word "our," but stayed silent.

"What would be important to you?" he asked.

"I think I'd want it a little way out of town. Not suburbia, but also not surrounded by farm fields."

"Agreed," he said. "I like the idea of a garage plus an out building. What style would we build?"

The "we" jumped at her this time. Where was he headed with this conversation?

"A small cottage, definitely," she said. "One with a downstairs floor plan that we could expand later."

"And, a wrap-around porch," he added. "I want to be able to read outside in the early evening."

This was definitely a new side of Russ. "What do you plan to read?"

"Bedtime stories to our kids," he said.

"Whoa!" she said. "How many kids are we having?"

"Maybe we better stick to looking at house plans for now," he said, "but, I want you in my future. Or, the other way around," he said, fearing he had pushed too hard, too fast.

"Could we have a slate roof?" she asked, seemingly out of nowhere.

"Do you know what those cost?" he asked in mock horror.

"It's not a deal breaker for me," she said. "I just wanted to see your reaction to a budget-busting request."

"I'm consistent," he said sheepishly.

"I like consistent."

"How 'bout we start checking the want ads for small acreage for sale?" he asked. "I'd want to be sure I could make you and Louise happy before I waltzed you down the aisle."

"And, I'd have to learn to waltz," she said.

"HEY, ERNIE," Russ said the next morning at work. "Thanks for the advice."

"Any time. Any time," Ernie said, and they never brought up the subject again.

"Not every living room needs a sofa. Loveseats and chairs give you flexibility for rearranging furniture by yourself on a rainy day."

30

Laura was late arriving for work. She had spent half an hour in the rain, trying to coax Louise to make the dash from a dry spot under the truck in the driveway to the front door. Louise had never responded well to the traditional "here kitty, kitty, kitty," apparently thinking he should be addressed more formally.

No matter how annoyed she was with Louise at the moment, Laura wasn't going to leave the spoiled cat outside on a rainy day. Though, she remembered, the weather reporter had said that showers would clear by 10 a.m. and Portlanders could expect bright sunshine by noon.

"Louise," she called. "Get up here or I'm eating the cat food I put out for you. I'm serious," she added for emphasis.

Louise could tell a bluff when he heard one, but he yielded anyway. He dashed past Laura in the doorway and went to the kitchen to make sure no one had nibbled on his breakfast.

Laura, whose hair had wilted while she was out in the rain trying to corral the cat, now reached for a lightweight rain coat, threw it on, and dashed out to the truck. She would be over forty minutes late for work.

"It's Russ' fault," she thought. "He gave me the damn cat."

Russ was at Graham Construction waiting for Laura when she rushed through the door. He was relieved to see her. He had resisted phoning to make sure she was safe.

"The drowned-rat look is fetching," he said lightly.

"Not in the mood," she answered. "If you hadn't given me that damned animal, I would have been here on time."

"Would that damned animal be loveable Louise?"

"One in the same," she answered. "Could we get right down to business here? I'm wet. I'm cold. And, I'm not in the best humor."

"Pardon me for breathing," he said.

"I'll take that under consideration."

"ARE YOU ACCEPTING calls of apology this evening?" the voice on Laura's phone said.

"Possibly," Laura answered. "Unless you're another telemarketer."

"I'm not selling anything," Russ said. "I called to ask you to dinner Friday night."

Laura softened a little. She had missed Russ. And, after talking with the police she was convinced what had looked like suspicious behavior while Russ was in New Jersey was actually a case of identity theft. Russ was still trying to unravel the credit card tangles to protect his personal credit rating and that of Graham Construction.

She thought she should give him a break. It wasn't his fault she hadn't been in the mood for humor that morning.

"What did you have in mind?" she asked.

"A late dinner at the Benson?" he asked. "After the happy hour crowd has left."

The words "I'd love to" came out of Laura's mouth before she knew she was going to say them.

"THIS CALLS FOR a shopping trip," Esther said when she heard that Laura and Russ had an actual date.

"I was thinking just the opposite," Laura said. "It's Russ. I see him every day. I won't have to fuss about how I look."

"Wrong."

"He sees me every day," Laura repeated.

"All the more reason to dress up," Esther said. "That's where married women go wrong. I should know," she said. "I've been married more times than most."

"We're going to the Benson Hotel for a late night dinner."

"Nice choice."

"So what do I wear at the end of a work day when I've sweat out any style my hair might have had when I left the house for work that morning?" Laura asked.

"Easy peasy," Esther answered. "Long black cocktail pants with a modified gladiator sandal. There are some nice, soft-pleated pants out this year."

"How do you know this stuff?"

"Combine those with a sheer black long-sleeved top with a v-neckline," Esther continued. "Not too low on the neckline. The sheer will add all the 'sexy' you need."

"And, where do I find this get up?" Laura asked.

"I saw it in a window downtown when I took the deposit to the bank this morning. It was a knockout on the mannequin. And her body wasn't half as good as yours."

"Thanks, but I don't know. I've got that dark green dress I wore last Christmas."

"You're missing the point. He's seen that," Esther said. "What size do you wear?" She didn't wait for an answer. "I'll drive back to that shop, get them to strip the mannequin and bring the pieces out for you to try."

"I don't know. How much was it?"

"Doesn't matter. Oh, and pull that beautiful auburn hair over in a loosely curled side pony tail Friday night."

Esther arrived at Laura's house after dinner, carrying the outfit on a bagged hanger. Laura was still amazed that Esther had asked to take the pants and blouse home on trial, but she'd known her to do much more outrageous things than that. Borrowing clothes from the biggest retailer in Portland paled compared to some of Esther's past escapades.

LAURA LOOKED at the label on the sheer top. "This is two sizes smaller than I usually buy," she said. "Are you sure I can get into it without busting a seam or something."

"Your bust will be fine," Esther assured her. "Better brands are roomier than your Target specials."

Laura wiggled into the slacks before she turned to see the entire ensemble in the mirror. "Whoa!" she said, repeating Russ' frequent response to her. "You've got to be kidding me."

"I told you it would fit," Esther said smugly.

"Can I get away with this neckline? If it were any lower, I'd have to wear a jewel in my navel."

She spun around twice more watching herself in the mirror. She was surprised to see that the v-neckline stayed snug against her skin and actually didn't expose any more than a bathing suit top might. Of course, she'd be above water while she was out with Russ.

"Relax," Esther said. "You aren't going to a middle school dance. He's invited you out for an intimate evening for two."

"This is intimate all right," Laura said, "but I like it."

"It's a side of you he's never seen."

"It's a side of me that no one should see outside the shower."

"So, are you wearing it or not?"

Laura leaned down and touched her toes. "I'm making sure it passes the I've-dropped-my-napkin test."

"How'd it do?"

"A-plus." Laura took a deep breath, looked at herself in the mirror for the sixth or seventh time and said, "I'm wearing this baby."

"Stand on your tiptoes," Esther ordered as Laura stood before her in the slinky pants and top. "Perfect," Esther said. "Will you have time to get new shoes tomorrow?"

"On my lunch hour?" Laura suggested meekly. She was a little overwhelmed by how fast the new clothes had transformed her from day laborer to night charmer.

"Do it," Esther said.

"I don't even know what all this costs," Laura said.

"Trust me. You don't want to," Esther said. "You'll have to wear the pieces separately several times for the next four years to justify the purchase. Just close your eyes and write the check."

LAURA WALKED BACK and forth in front of the full-length mirror which hung on the back of her bedroom door at The Harrington. She didn't look like the same woman when she was wearing the black outfit. It was as if she'd turned into a new and improved—and definitely taller and sleeker—model of her own self. She loved feeling this way.

She remembered she'd felt a little tongue-tied around Russ when she first joined Graham Construction Company. He was what college age girls used to call "a hunk." She wondered if that expression was still in vogue. Russ was definitely still in shape. And, the year-round construction worker tan added to the rugged look. Only she and Esther knew what a softy he was inside.

The doorbell rang and Louise dashed up the stairs and then followed Laura back down, batting at the swinging pant legs as Laura moved toward the front door. She opened it with the chain lock still in place—a skill Pfeifer had taught her—and peeked out to see Russ standing there in a sport coat and tie.

"Do you plan to let me in?" he asked.

"Louise and I are still deciding," she said as she slid the chain lock out of the catch and opened the door.

"Wow."

There should have been something more appropriate than "wow," but Russ was speechless. So he said it again. The word had the advantage of being said either backwards or forwards, he thought.

"Wow."

"Thank you," Laura said.

"You look great. You also look hungry," he said awkwardly as he scanned the tall sleek figure in front of him. "I think we'll have dodged the traffic coming home from work so it shouldn't take us long to get there."

He helped her out the door, using his foot to keep Louise from scampering out to join them.

He was glad to see that she had a light coat with her and he helped her into it. He wasn't sure he was man enough to fight off all the men on the street who would be doing a double take at the knockout auburn-haired woman in black who would be on his arm as they approached the hotel restaurant. Once they were inside and she had checked her coat, if he needed help, he could call on reinforcements from the wait staff.

THE WAITER SUGGESTED a bottle of wine, but both Russ and Laura remembered that wine was not her best friend. It took very little to send her head swimming.

"I think we'd like to start with individual glasses," Russ said to the disappointed waiter. "If you'll give us a couple minutes, we'll be ready to order."

The waiter wandered off and they looked over the menu. Everything looked good to Laura. Russ ordered a steak and she finally zeroed in on a half-size chicken parmesan meal with "delicately seasoned pasta." As if by magic, the waiter returned the minute they had decided and placed the order for them.

When Laura turned to watch the server walk away, the light caught the gold oval hoop earrings she was wearing.

"I like your earrings," Russ said. "I was going to wait, but maybe I should give you this now," he said as he passed a small gift box over to her.

"What's this? I didn't forget my own birthday, did I?" Laura asked.

"It's something I had made for you before I left for hurricane duty. I asked Esther to keep it safe for me while I was gone."

Laura opened the box and saw a chain with a heart-shaped pendant. The locket had a stylized cursive letter L on it, with rubies set along the curves of the letter. It hung from a delicate gold chain.

"It's breath-taking," Laura told him. She opened the small catch on the locket and found that Russ had added two tiny photos inside. One of Louise on one side, and a photo of Hammer on the other. It was the perfect touch.

He leaned across the table and kissed her lightly—just as the waiter arrived with the salads.

"Well that broke the moment," Russ said.

He helped her put on the necklace which filled in the v-neckline on her blouse perfectly. She realized that

Esther had handpicked the outfit to go with the gift. "You go, Esther," she thought.

As they finished dinner, she reached up and fingered the necklace again.

"I've never seen anything as beautiful as this," she said.

"There's not another one like it," he explained. "I had the idea in my head, but we both know I'm not the designer on this team. Charmaigne helped me sketch it.

"Then, I went to that jeweler who's been on Main Street in Lake Oswego for years. He crafted the necklace." Russ said. "I can't believe Charmaigne kept her mouth shut and didn't spoil this for me."

"I'm confused," Laura said. "If you had this planned, why did you tell me to date other guys?"

"I did nothing of the kind."

"You certainly did," she said. "You said I should. . ."

"I meant don't sit home alone," he interrupted. "Stay over at Esther's once in a while. Call an old girlfriend and go to a movie . . ."

"Oh," she said. "Actually, Charmaigne did blab. She said you were over at her place often. I'm afraid I thought the worst."

"You didn't! Charmaigne with me! My God, woman," he said in disbelief.

"Sorry," Laura said meekly.

"I wasn't sure we were ready for a ring, but I wanted to give you something to remind you that I'm seriously taken by you." He leaned forward.

With perfect timing, the waiter arrived and slid the dessert menus between them and onto the center of the candlelit table.

Seriously taken? Those weren't the words a woman wanted to hear.

Russ knew the second the words left his lips that it hadn't been what he meant to say at all.

"That came out wrong," he said.

"It's OK," she said. "It's going to take me a little while to get rid of all the anger I stored up those three weeks."

"I understand."

"I'm not sure you do," she said. "There's 'mad' and then there's 'hurt 'n mad.'"

"I'd never hurt you," he said. He hesitated, then added, "I get the strong feeling I'm in trouble here," he said. "Do you still feel anything for me?"

"I love you," she said simply. "We need more time is all."

"I'll run with your first three words."

"Aren't you the one who taught me to always read the fine print?" she asked, lightening the mood.

"I'm also the one who told you to not worry things to death," he said. "Seize the moment." He leaned across the table, planning to kiss her long and lovingly. On cue, the waiter returned to take their dessert order.

"Why don't we take it one day at a time?" Laura asked.

"One day at a time," Russ repeated. This time they weren't interrupted when he leaned over and kissed her on the lips. To hell with the waiter.

CHARMAIGNE INVITED the Grahams and Laura to tour the home she had decorated next door to the Italianate house. Laura and Esther had grown more and more curious about the interior of that house as the months had gone by at the Street of Dreams. Russ begged off from the invitation, but the women jumped at the chance to see what the designer had created next door.

They returned thirty minutes later, hoping they had chosen all the right words as they stood awed by the vivid colors and elaborate furnishings Charmaigne had selected.

"You were very polite, Esther," Laura said. "I appreciate that."

"That house is one hot mess."

"Charmaigne simply has a different style of decorating than the rest of us," Laura tried. "Though, that family room bordered on ugly."

"It looked like a flat I stayed in once in Belgium," Esther said. "At first glance it 'bordered on ugly.' Then it got damn ugly."

"Charmaigne does have an intriguing way of combining colors," Laura said, still straining for tact and diplomacy.

"It's like she picked the colors from a Chinese menu. One choice from column A, two from Column B . . ."

"How was your tour? What'd I miss?" Russ asked as he joined the women.

"The egg rolls," Esther said without further explanation.

"There are three feet in a yard—and one in a paint tray if you step sideways while painting."

31

"Laura's upstairs taking her frustration out on the kids' room. She blames herself for all the troubles we've encountered on this job," Esther said as she and Russ heard the sound of a sledge hammer bouncing off the remains of the partitions in the bedroom upstairs.

"You don't believe that, do you?" Russ asked Esther.

"The jury's still out where I'm concerned."

"You're kidding me," Russ said.

"Of course, I don't really believe it," Esther said. "But if I was outside in a lightning storm with Laura and twenty six other people lined up from A to Z behind her, I'd stand behind number Z. Wherever Laura goes, trouble finds her."

RUSSELL GRAHAM HADN'T wanted to worry Aunt Esther or Laura by sharing his concerns before now. But, if they were to be a team, he knew he had to be forthcoming. In hindsight, he regretted taking the time off to go back East in the middle of the project.

"Do you remember the day we first toured this site?" he asked. "It was a hillside villa with the one house and fields and fields of wildflowers."

"Of course," Esther said. "I was against it because the terrain was so rocky and I turned my ankle. I was annoyed and I took it out on the house."

"The wildflowers were like nothing I'd ever seen before, covering the entire site," Russ said.

"What are you getting at?" Laura asked.

"It took less than six months to turn all that into a high crime neighborhood. And nobody's living here yet."

"You're exaggerating," Laura said.

"Not so much," he said. "We've had our share of calamities. Count 'em off."

"Well, there was Mr. Martinelli, of course," Esther said. "Do you two ever regret that we didn't get to meet him?"

"No," they said in unison.

"Well, I'm glad we went to the service," Esther recalled.

"Keep counting," Russ said.

"There's the HOA," Laura said.

"That's the truth, but I don't think we can put it on the Calamity List," Esther said.

"I think we have to omit my New Jersey misfortune, too," Russ added. "But, there's still plenty to go around here. Keep listing."

"I almost got a ticket on the way home from the airport."

"You did?" Russ asked.

"Charmaigne got beat up," Esther said.

"Not exactly," Laura thought.

"And you got trapped in the pantry," she said aloud. "It was the same weekend that someone threw red paint on the house."

"That was 'stupidity,' not 'calamity.' There's a major difference."

"Hell, Laura got hit by a cement truck," Russ put in.

"The fireplace imploded and the carriage house burned down with that poor woman inside. And, then we lost Jamen Childers," Laura said sadly. Esther put an arm around Laura's shoulder.

"This conversation started with the beautiful wildflowers. How'd we get here?" Esther asked.

Russ admitted that he had led them through the review of the events of the last months to see if they could figure out if there was a common thread to what had happened. If he were the detective assigned out here, he'd be searching for "commonalities" between the events.

"So," he said, "are we dealing with one wild-eyed criminal here or are these events all unrelated?"

The room was quiet. Finally, Esther spoke. "There's no way to tell. I say we just keep taking it day by day."

Russ and Laura exchanged glances. It was clear to them both that their minds were now on that romantic dinner they shared rather than the murder and mayhem on the Street of Dreams.

Russ remained quiet, brooding about how insane the things were on this year's Street of Dreams. The onus of responsibility for keeping Laura and Aunt Esther safe was his, and he hoped he'd be able to handle the job.

"Be sure you've got your cell phones with you at all times," he said. "Charged."

Esther patted her pocket. The phone was filed between her X-acto knife and tape measure.

ESTHER'S VIEWS ON technology had softened some, but she was still not a fan. She'd seen no indication yet of the earlier promise those in technology fields had made that computers would reduce the number of sheets of paper that crossed her desk. If anything the piles were deeper.

Her computer was operating smoothly today, but the new printer was driving her crazy. She'd been frustrated enough when she learned that, instead of two ink cartridges, this newer model required a different cartridge for each ink color. And, of course, none of those little ink jets ran out on the same day. While she admired the competitive blue one which consistently won the game, she secretly thanked the yellow one for not needing to be subbed as often.

"If I believed in reincarnation, would I have to come back as something living?" Esther asked Laura.

"Why? Do you believe in reincarnation?"

"Just asking," Esther answered. "I'm thinking of coming back as a computer printer." She stretched out in her chair and balanced her feet lightly on the coffee table in the main room at Graham Construction.

"Why would you want to do that?"

"Isn't it obvious? If I were this damned printer, I'd only have to work when I wanted to. I could quit at any time without notice. Beach trip!"

Laura held her tongue.

"If I got frustrated, I could spew papers out of sequence all over the floor and somebody else would have to pick 'em up. And, to aggravate those around me, I'd be sure to run out of ink five minutes after employees at Staples locked the doors."

"Could I help you with something?" Laura asked.

"Yeah. See if Mr. Underwood is on *Match.com?* I was compatible with him."

"Grandma's refurbished old trunk will make a lovely coffee table. Just be sure you know where Fluffy was buried before opening the trunk."

32

Staging a house was one of the more exciting parts of the job for Laura. Her methods differed from professional "house stagers" plumping up family homes to appeal to the greatest number of buyers. Laura knew she was lucky because, in her line of work, she always started with a house that wasn't occupied. It gave her a clean canvas from which to work.

With the Italianate house, though, her canvas wasn't snowy white. Each room already had a background of muted soft colors set off by the original wood window surrounds or glossy white chair rails, crown molding and baseboards.

The window placements in the kids' bedrooms and master bedroom dictated how the furniture would be arranged, but Laura couldn't wait to get her hands on the downstairs areas.

There were three standard arrangements for living room furniture, and she knew each relied on facing the primary seating pieces toward a focal point. That focal point could be a view out a window, a warm glowing fireplace, a dramatic piece or artwork, or even Grandma's antique melodeon. Just so the person seated on that couch would have something interesting to look at if conversation lagged or he had already read the copy of *Sunset* displayed on the low table in front of the couch.

Laura could "order in" the furniture from the best stores and boutiques in the area for a small fee as long as she named the stores on a list of sources for furnishings that would be handed out at the realtors' open house tour. Future buyers sometimes made offers on the Street of Dreams houses complete with the furniture as shown. Both the builders and the furniture dealers won on that deal.

Laura had tried two different arrangements for the living room. She faced the oversized sofa across from the fireplace which she flanked with two arm chairs. As she moved a rectangular glass sofa table into the tableau, she was already nixing the arrangement.

"Too stale," she said aloud.

Then, she floated the sofa in the room and placed the backs of the chairs on each side of the window with an oversized lamp table between them.

"Charming but boring," she said, now breathless from having shoved the overstuffed pieces around the room on her collection of little brown portable plastic casters.

Finally, she picked up the phone and dialed the owner at a store in the Pearl District. He offered to pick up the original couch and two chairs the next day and deliver two chic modern couches upholstered in soft cream velvet.

When they arrived, Laura set the new couches lengthwise, facing each other in front of the fireplace. They were separated by a large floating glass tabletop with a weathered driftwood sculpture supporting it. The arrangement made the living room look expansive and upscale. She added a beveled mirror with a pounded metal frame on the wall opposite the fireplace. She flanked the mirror with large potted palms.

As an afterthought, she added a sofa table with two small accent lamps behind one of the couches. And, Laura's first staged room downstairs was complete.

She worked two more days staging the remaining downstairs rooms. To the unsuspecting house hunter, it looked like a very sophisticated (and incredibly tidy) young Portland society couple and their offspring could buy and occupy the house within an hour. The dining table was elegantly set and ready for that family's evening meal.

"Probably a catered cheese, artichoke and pine nut pasta served with a salad of garden-fresh greens and grilled shrimp," Laura thought.

Moving is always soooo exhausting.

The bathrooms now sported soft fluffy white towels. There were glass candle holders on the tub surround in the master bath. She had even scattered a few pull toys and brightly colored books in the children's bedrooms to both showcase the décor and keep the little ones occupied while their parents weighed the pros and cons of handling a mammoth mortgage to live here.

RUSS AND ESTHER came in to the dining room to take a look at Laura's staging efforts in the large elegant space.

"The chairs don't match," Esther said, surveying the dining room table.

"That's on purpose," Laura said.

"I learn something every day," Esther said.

"Hey, I've had that look for years at my place," Russ added.

Laura stopped fussing with the table settings and turned to explain.

"I don't like identical chairs. It can look like sextuplets all dressed alike for Sunday school."

"Go on," Russ said hesitantly.

"The trick to making this work is to have the chairs at the heads of the table different from the others," she said. "Or, you can have each chair different as long as they're from the same vintage or the same color or wood finish."

"I'd do that and it would look like a hodgepodge," Esther said. "This looks great."

"There's a little more to it," Laura added. "If you look closely, you'll see that all the chairs are within two inches in height. Plus, I used the same fabric when I recovered all the cushions. That unifies it."

"I don't know about 'unifying,' but I know this room looks great," Russ said.

"Until some kid spills spaghetti sauce on the cushion," Esther added.

"Scotch Guard," Laura said simply.

"I once dated someone in the Scotch Guard," Esther said, letting her voice trail off as she moved toward the kitchen.

"Glass table tops are an elegant choice to visually expand the size of a room. If you purchase one, also buy stock in Windex."

33

Esther was moving from one potted plant to the next on her roof garden, giving each a morning shot of water. The only negative to a roof top garden, she thought, was that underground drip systems weren't possible. She deadheaded the climbing Cecil Bruner rose bush that she'd been told would never thrive in a wooden pot.

"We showed them," she told the bush. The rosebush had covered the entire back of the trellis, giving her a private hideaway.

She'd been hearing for years that houseplants thrived better if you talked to them, but she didn't believe it. She brought hers home from the nursery, sat them near a window and said "grow or you're history." Except for last year's Boston fern, they had all taken her warning to heart.

Her roof-top flower garden consisted primarily of fuchsias in baskets shaded by the trellis. She also had a potted vegetable and herb garden. She limited the veggies to Early Girl and Oregon Star tomatoes, which grew up the wire teepees in their pots, and to three different kinds of peppers.

"It's a taco garden," she had explained to Russ when he asked about the selections.

Esther often had her early-morning coffee and breakfast in the roof garden surrounded by the plants, but she had yet to engage in a serious conversation with any of them.

It was already warm this morning, and the weather channel had promised temperatures up to 100 degrees today. This was not unheard of for early August in Portland, but it was unusual enough to call for special news breaks on Channel 8 off and on last evening.

Esther's bow to the predictions was to fix a glass of iced tea instead of coffee to wash down her morning maple bar. Actually she ate two. With cream filling.

"Everyone's entitled to a vice or two," she said to the sweet basil plant. She had a small table and chair set in this terrace area, but sat today in one of the white Adirondack chairs she'd adorned with soft cream and persimmon chevron-pattern pillows.

"See," Esther said to none of the plants in particular, "if I hadn't met Laura, I would have thought those pillows were red with wiggly white stripes."

She let her thoughts wander to the project that was nearing completion on the Street of Dreams. The restoration project had started in spring and was finishing up with all the show houses ready for tours the end of August. For a group of contractors who barely knew each other when the foundations were poured, she thought, the group had melded well.

Her thoughts shifted to Jamen Childers, the late Jamen Childers. The police who came to the house had all but confirmed that the young man had taken his own life. Esther, though, as a former emergency room nurse, found it interesting that they had never mentioned the method of his demise. The obituary had also been brief.

Maybe that was a courtesy to Mrs. Childers who had lost her only child. Or, maybe the police hadn't formally closed the investigation yet.

"Or," she thought, "maybe all those years of dealing with violent deaths at the hospital turned me into a ghoul."

She wasn't the only one who wondered. Laura had asked also, and then chastised Esther for guessing "designer pills."

ESTHER WAS SITTING at her computer at Graham Construction, waiting for Russ to come downstairs and for Laura to walk up the block and check in before going out to the Dreams house. Since retiring from her emergency room job in Seattle and forming the company with Russ, Esther had been the one who took care of the finances for the operation.

She was concerned. With all the negative publicity, and now only six houses to be completed on the Dreams Street, there would be fewer visitors, fewer paid admissions to the open house days, and fewer zeros in the prices that the realtors would recommend for the remaining listings.

She had an idea, but she needed to run it past the other two partners. She suspected Laura would be an easy sell, but Russ was more contemplative and aware of deadlines on their own project. She knew both of them had to go along before she could suggest her plan to the other building teams.

"WART WAS BY here last week to remind us again that he is a licensed Realtor and hopes to get the listing on our place and all the others," Laura said.

"What did you tell him?" Esther asked.

"I was afraid to say 'bite me,'" Laura answered. But, it turned out that 'in your dreams' wasn't a very good choice either."

"Is that guy bothering you two?" Russ asked.

"Do cows moo?"

Russ and Laura looked at Esther, wondering where that expression had come from. What they had to remember about Esther is that if you asked, she'd answer. One way or another. They didn't ask.

"He's a jerk," Laura said bluntly. "Here's your test. I heard Charmaigne tell him the other day that if he came on their property again she'd be armed and shoot low."

"Ouch," Ernie said as he entered the room.

"I had an idea while I was sitting in the garden and I think it's worth sharing." Esther said.

The other three waited.

"The exterior of Francesca's place appears to be complete. I think we ought to talk to the other teams and see if we could all pitch in and landscape the place," Esther said. "I know Jamen was way ahead of the rest of us in decorating the interior. If the builders would take care of minimal landscaping, maybe the decorators could each choose a room over there and complete the interior."

"They overbuilt that lot by so much that landscaping shouldn't be a major deal," Laura volunteered.

"Are you feeling sentimental, Aunt Essie?" Russ asked softly

"Hell no," she said. "I'm looking at the bottom line, the same one that every other builder out here is probably losing sleep over every night since Jamen Childers died. Am I the only one who didn't see that suicide coming?"

"Should we share this idea with the association and their man Simmons before we talk to the others?" Russ asked.

"You bring Wart into this discussion and I walk," Laura said.

"Right behind you, Sistah," Esther said, bringing back a phrase from her days marching for women's rights.

"Let me be r-e-a-l-l-y clear here," Laura said. "If the builders and decorators are willing to pitch in to save this outfit, the association ought to do its part. I say we tell them this plan is only a 'go' if they pull Wart off the job?"

"Remind me never to get on the wrong side of you two," Russ said.

"I assumed you knew that already," Ernie said.

WHEN LAURA SPOTTED Ward Simmons walking across the Dreams property toward the house, she went into the back bathroom downstairs and closed the door. She wasn't sure the move would work because her truck was parked in the drive, but maybe he'd think she had left with Esther in the Element.

It always made Laura smile when she saw Esther arrive, often with Hammer riding shotgun, the dog letting the wind come in through the windows and blow his ears back.

Since Russ's return, Ernie didn't arrive until later in the day. Laura reminded herself to thank Russ for keeping Ernie on the payroll. He was a fine addition to the crew. And if she ever wanted to fly to the moon, she'd check with Ernie for reservations.

"Laura," she heard Simmons call out.

Laura froze. She was not taking time out of her day to hear another tirade on how much more money everyone could make if they all went in together and listed their properties with one Edward Simmons. She wouldn't dream of touring an empty house with him along as the agent. She couldn't imagine any other woman in Portland would feel differently. And, everyone agreed women made the final decision on most house purchases. Men might like a property, but women had universal veto power.

She could hear him walking around on the floor downstairs. She made a decision, lifted the lower half of the bathroom window, and lowered herself to the side yard. It was a quick sprint to her truck and she was backing out and headed to Taco Bell for their 99 cent special pink lemonade freeze. If others could take a coffee break, she could take a freeze break as often as she wanted to avoid their on-site real estate shark.

She had been sitting outside at The Bell at a table shaded by an umbrella for less than five minutes when Charmaigne's Mercedes pulled into the parking lot. Char got out and walked over to where Laura was sitting.

"I followed you," she said.

"So I see."

"When I saw you slide down the outside of the house, I thought something must be really wrong. But, then I heard Mr. Simmons calling you and I decided wherever you were going, I was going too. I can't stand that man."

"Well, hallelujah," Laura thought. Maybe she'd been too hard on Charmaigne. They actually had something in common.

Laura felt herself soften toward the other woman. She told Char about Esther's idea to complete Jamen's house and Charmaigne began to cry softly.

"Do you think we could actually do that? That would mean so much to me," she said. "And I know Jamen's plans. He had chosen a palette of pale blues, soft grays, and metallics for the entire house. We could all interpret that individually, but the whole house would have a unified décor."

"So you'd be 'in'?" Laura asked.

"Abso-effen-lutely," Char said. "I loved Jamen. I'd have taken a bullet for that man, if it wouldn't have killed me."

Charmaigne's enthusiasm—strange as it may be—was a good thing since Russ was visiting with the head of the builders' association this morning. Charmaigne had opted for the lime freeze drink which she claimed tasted like a "naked margarita."

"If you know what I mean," she said.

AFTER MUCH DISCUSSION, the builders on the Street of Dreams decided Russ and Laura would be the appropriate ones to approach Francesca Childers with the offer of help.

When the delegation of two described the number of people who were willing to pitch in to help Mrs. Childers complete her house, the woman softened before their eyes. Laura thought Francesca Childers might cry.

Francesca, however, recovered quickly and spoke in a controlled voice when she accepted the offer of help.

"I accept the offer. It's what Jamen would have wanted," she said. "Tell the volunteers to spare no expense on materials," she added. "The bills should be sent to me. It will be my last gift to Jamen."

"Grass cloth is back. By the time you've paid in full for this expensive wallpaper, though, it will be time to start stripping it."

34

Officer Anderson pulled the patrol car to the curb in front of the Italianate house. He and the detective had always thought their own work was tedious until they watched the restoration process at the Street of Dreams. Whatever profit Graham Construction made on the project wouldn't be enough, he thought.

Since Jamen Childers' death, Anderson's work load had doubled.

"Quadrupled," Detective Roberts corrected. "I had hoped we'd never have to talk to Francesca Childers again. No such luck."

When they hadn't found Mrs. Childers at her project home, they moved down the block where they saw Laura's truck parked in front of the old house.

"The porch looks good," Anderson said.

They found Laura outside, painting the smaller side porch.

"Any idea where we'd find Mrs. Childers?" the officer asked.

"An easy question this time."

"Does it have an answer?" Detective Roberts asked.

"Esther, Charmaigne and Mrs. Childers should be at Francesca's house up the block. They're trying to agree on the design concept for a sign for the front of this development," she said.

"Good luck on that," Officer Anderson said.

Apparently, Mrs. Childers had elected not to open the door when she had seen their police car in front of her house earlier.

They circled back on foot and found the three women in the room that showed as "lady's office" on the floor plan for Francesca's lavish new house. Officer Anderson noticed that the Childers' house was nearer completion than the others on the block. Jamen had tacked paint strips to the walls and distributed flooring samples among the downstairs rooms before his death. He had covered the upstairs floors with luxurious, thick, snow white carpeting earlier.

Even Detective Roberts, who lived alone in an old downtown apartment, recognized that the décor would be top grade when the house was completed.

But, he wasn't there to second guess some decorator.

"Late decorator," he thought.

Mrs. Childers welcomed them and re-introduced them to Esther and Charmaigne, as though none of them had met in the past.

The detective explained that additional questions had come up since the medical examiner's report on Jamen Childers' death.

"Do you have time to answer those questions now or would you like to come down to the Bureau?" he asked.

"I can't believe it will take that long," Francesca said. "I told you everything I know last time you two were here. If you keep harassing me, I'm going to consider filing a complaint."

Roberts ignored the tone of her response and suggested that the women reschedule their discussion so he and Anderson could talk with Mrs. Childers privately in the expansive home's office space.

"There's no reason for them to leave," she said. "As I said, this will be brief."

"Would you ladies care to wait in another part of the house?" he asked. "I suspect Mrs. Childers is too polite to tell you that she will need some privacy."

"Of course," Charmaigne said. "We'll be on the other side of the wall here if you need us, Francesca."

The older woman glared at the use of her first name by someone she considered beneath her social station in life. Esther followed Charmaigne out the door without comment.

THE INTERVIEW began abruptly with Francesca's voice echoing through the near empty house.

"My father started it."

"Mrs. Childers, when we're looking at a crime as serious as murder, we don't expect to hear the grade school playground defense of 'he started it.'"

"Don't patronize me, Detective Roberts," she said. "My grandfather was Langston Childers, a highly respected banker and land developer in Portland before the Great Depression washed across the country."

"And your point would be?"

"Detective, I'm no longer conversing with you. I'll talk to this young officer who appears to have been taught proper manners." She turned to Will Anderson and continued.

"Grandfather retired from banking before the financial crash, not this recent mere blip in the economy," she said. She paused for emphasis. "Grandfather saw *The* Depression coming and he couldn't bear to see his depositors left destitute. He was a kind and caring individual. The dear man's only error in a prosperous and respected career was to let my father inherit the family land investments upon Grandfather's death."

"Could we get to the point?" the detective asked.

"Please remind the detective that I am not speaking to him."

"Please continue, Mrs. Childers," Officer Anderson said.

"When I, in turn, inherited the land from my father—including the very land, I might remind you, this lucrative development sits upon today—I immediately hired a real estate management company to oversee the various investments. I had little interest in the 'family dirt' as my late mother used to call the real estate in this area.

"Of course, I didn't know then to what she referred." A single tear rolled down Francesca Childers' right cheek.

"We've been rude," the officer said. "I apologize. I know this is extremely difficult for you, Mrs. Childers. Would you like to take a break? Could we get you a cup of coffee?"

"Tea would be lovely," she said. "I can't take a break or I will never get this said. And, it's time for the story to come to an end. Those poor, poor girls," she said, sniffing and dabbing her nose with a lace trimmed handkerchief.

"You lost me."

"Pay attention, Officer. Don't let yourself be like the detective here," she said as she accepted a cup of hot tea from Roberts. No one dared ask how he had produced a teabag, china cup and saucer instead of the usual Oregon 3R (reduce-reuse-recycle) cardboard cup.

"Mrs. Childers, I'm going to ask Officer Anderson to read you your Miranda rights before I let you proceed." Roberts said.

"He can read them, but I waive them," she replied.

"Listen to every word carefully," Anderson said. "Waiving your rights may not be in your best interest." Anderson recited her rights and explained that she could call an attorney.

"Enough," Mrs. Childers said. "You read them. I listened to them. I waive them."

"Shall we go ahead?" Anderson asked. Roberts nodded.

"I never visited any of the properties. It simply wasn't an interest of mine," Mrs. Childers began. "Unfortunately, the firm I hired, didn't tour the investment properties in person either. They collected the rents, oversaw yard maintenance, kept track of tax statements," she said, her voice trailing off.

"Oregon has dreadfully high property taxes," she said to no one in particular.

The police waited for her to continue.

"My surprise came three and a half years ago when I contacted my late father's accountant and confidential friend about possibly selling the property to the local builders' association. He explained that the family mansion was then rented and bringing in thousands of dollars a month to my personal accounts."

"And?"

"In short, I discovered that my father had used that elegant Italianate house, my grandmother's dream home, as a holding place for young girls who had ventured against their will into prostitution."

"The sex trade?" asked the detective.

"Don't use that vulgar term," she snapped.

"You'd prefer 'house of ill repute?'"

"Get him out of my sight!" Her face had turned crimson and she ran her hands wildly through her newly coifed hair.

"I didn't know. I didn't know," Francesca wailed.

"And," Anderson asked gently. "What did you do when you found out?"

"I closed down the operation, young man. Without delay," she said. "Each woman there at the time was given money orders for the cost of six month's housing, a stipend for living expenses, and a very carefully worded letter of recommendation for employment in another field. It was the best I could do."

"You could have called the cops," Detective Roberts said.

"You ninny. I could do nothing of the kind. Unknowingly, I had been living on the gains from those girls and others like them throughout my childhood and all these years since my father's passing."

Officer Anderson pulled a printed card out of his pocket. "There's no hurry here," he said. "Why don't you take a few minutes to review the rights printed on this card?" he asked Mrs. Childers.

She took the card, dropped it on the floor, and kicked it aside, crushing it like a cigarette butt.

"Let me guess," the detective said. "Our friend Sal Martinelli knew about the house and began blackmailing you."

"Precisely. The garlic-breathed little slug."

"Mrs. Childers, please tell me that wasn't a reference to Mr. Martinelli's Italian heritage. In Oregon, there are additional penalties if the prosecuting attorney can prove that a death was a hate crime."

"Of course it wasn't a racial slur. It was a comment based upon the drunken little weasel breathing right in my face. I was simply going to threaten him with the gun, but he leaned in real close and called me 'Frannie' as though I were one of those girls kept at the house."

"And you shot him?"

"Twice," she said. "Mother always stressed thoroughness when performing a task."

THE DETECTIVE CALLED a halt to the interview to give Mrs. Childers a chance to compose herself. He stayed with her and Anderson stepped through the door to the other room where he found Esther and Charmaigne seated in the only two occasional chairs in an otherwise empty space. From the tracks on the subfloor, he could tell that they had inched their way toward the wall separating the rooms so they would be able to hear more clearly as the interview moved forward. He couldn't blame them.

If Mrs. Childers had wanted the two women to stay, who was he to send them packing? With an off-site interview like this, it might work to the police advantage to have witnesses. Had Detective Roberts had any idea what Mrs. Childers was going to divulge,

Anderson knew he would have summoned her to the Bureau for the interview.

Now, he suspected they were ahead to stay put and not break the flow of her statement. They had the hand-held recorder with them. He'd see if she would agree to that.

"She confessed to killing Sal Martinelli," Esther said in disbelief.

"Maybe it was some strange psychological grief reaction after Jamen's death," Charmaigne suggested. "Why would she confess to murder? How can we tell if she really did it?"

"There's no telling," Esther said. "Her story sure puts a different slant on those three cell-sized rooms we found and. . ."

"Nobody told me about any cells," Char interrupted.

". . . evidence of someone trying to remove mortar from the inside of the fireplace."

"Do you think she killed that man?"

"There's no telling," Esther repeated.

"There's one way of telling," Anderson said as he looked at the two women. "Detective Roberts never released the information that Martinelli died from two bullet wounds," he said. "Mrs. Childers just told us she shot him twice."

Anderson excused himself and returned to the makeshift interview room where Mrs. Childers was standing, staring out the double-paned picture window.

Detective Roberts spoke first.

"We'd like to resume our earlier conversation, Mrs. Childers, about your right to an attorney. We're not sure you've made a wise decision."

"It's my choice, not yours," she said. "It's impossible to make everyone happy. If I'd chopped Martinelli up in little pieces first, the Howard woman would have griped about the pink tint to the cement."

The officer looked dumbstruck.

"Now what?" she asked.

"The deceased was someone's son," he said. "Think of your own recent loss."

"We have a job to do here, but we try to show some respect," Detective Roberts added.

"I've spent my entire life being respectful. What do you say we give it a rest?"

Her questioners were at a momentary loss for words.

Detective Roberts recovered his voice first. "For accuracy, would you mind if we used this recorder to keep a record of the remainder of the interview?" he asked.

"Fine with me," she said. "I have a very good lawyer."

"Call him," Anderson said.

Roberts flipped the recorder switch to "on."

"As we've told you twice before, Mrs. Childers, you have the right to have an attorney present," he began. "Before we ask additional questions, I would advise you to call one or, at the very least, we could conclude this interview until you can have your attorney present for our questions."

Mrs. Childers ignored the advice again with a wave of her hand.

Roberts spoke into the recorder noting the names of those present, the date, time and place of the interview. "Those present include Detective Leonard Roberts, Officer William Anderson, and Mrs. Francesca Childers."

"Do *I* get to ask any questions here?" Mrs. Childers asked. "What about the hand?"

"We may never know," the detective said. "We now suspect whoever you hired to dispose of Martinelli's body exposed the hand either to taunt you or to draw public attention to the crime scene," he said. "Could that have been your son?"

"My son! He didn't play football, he didn't date women, and he definitely didn't have the guts to touch a corpse," she said.

"So who did you ask?"

"I asked my son. Just like you said. But, he wouldn't do it."

"Good for him."

"For once in his life, I thought Jamen might have a backbone," she said. "I told him I could not have the family name involved in a public scandal, and he wouldn't even do this one little favor for his mother. He never did understand the honor bestowed upon him when he became a Childers."

"Who helped you?"

"The Childers women have always had to be strong," she said. "Let's just say the body was completely covered when I left."

"Do you think your son returned to the scene?"

"You're the detective here."

"Let's get back to the hand," Roberts said.

"Hands. Plural," she corrected him. "I suspect the old dude."

The detective looked confused. "Mr. Gallo?"

"No," she said. "H.H., Harmless Homeless, that creature Mrs. Graham befriended. My guess is it was a bumbled attempt by him to save one of his own kind."

"Since you brought it up, how about the mannequin's hand?" he asked.

"A desperate act. Well below my usual standards," she apologized. "I was trying anything and everything to get Graham Constructions to tear down that house. They were beyond stubborn."

Detective Roberts took the seat across from her and leaned in closer.

"Was there something else you wanted to tell us?" he asked.

"What's the use? I'm obviously going to have to do all the 'detecting' here," she said. "You disappoint me, Detective. Jamen was a disappointment to me, too," she said. "Even in his early years."

"And?"

"Later all he had to do was back the cement truck over Laura Howard. He wasn't even man enough to do that. He pretended he didn't see her swerve at the last minute," she said with disgust.

"Maybe if I'd named him Harley like his father wanted. . ."

THAT WAS ALL Charmaigne could take. She stepped forward, opened the door, and slid into the home office before anyone could object. Esther hovered in the doorway.

"Didn't date women?" Char asked. "Didn't date women? Jamen and I have been an item since before this project started. He's the main reason I signed on."

"Oh, spare me the dramatics," Francesca Childers said.

"The 'gay decorator' was an act we created to irritate you."

"No! Not you and my Jamen."

"I don't think you're entitled to the details of our relationship, Mrs. Childers, but trust me. Jamen was incredibly well-versed in the skills required for *your* family business."

Francesca's jaw clenched and her face reddened. Officer Anderson tightened his grip on her arm.

"Liar!" Francesca yelled. "You didn't know him like I did. At the end, he couldn't even kill himself without help."

Charmaigne backed away.

"Don't look at me like I'm a murderer," the older woman said. "When I got there he had already dripped blood all over that glorious white frieze carpet. There's no way that will come out."

Detective Roberts grasped her other arm.

"When I found him he was as white as that rug. He kept saying 'help me, help me' in this pitiful tone. The carpet was already ruined. So I did as requested. I cut the second wrist for him."

The Detective debated whether to tell her now or later that the Medical Examiner had ruled that the first wrist injury would not have been fatal.

"Francesca," Anderson said. "May I call you Francesca?"

"It's Mrs. Childers," she corrected him.

"Mrs. Childers, I'm concerned about your attitude. You may be looking at two counts of Aggravated Murder," he said. "With the right attorney you might get those two counts . . ."

"Three counts," Detective Roberts corrected him.

"Ahhhh, the detective can 'detect' after all," the woman said. "Tell us more, Detective. We want to know how clever you are."

"I'm guessing if we checked your fingerprints against some partials that we found on the two gas cans hidden near the carriage house that burned on the Dreams Street, we might find something interesting."

"I don't know how interesting it would be," she said. "I mean in the realm of other things we're talking about it hardly makes the list."

"Why don't you tell us about that night?"

"I was moving the gas cans from my garage to the Graham place. I planned to wait for the opportune time. I'm seldom indecisive, but making the decision to burn down my grandparents' home took some thought. All the family heirlooms had been moved out and disposed of long ago, but the house still held some memories."

Anderson nodded.

"I had moved the first can into the structure when I heard someone stumbling around in there. I wasn't sure if it was that incompetent Simmons creature or someone else," she said. "If I were the detective here, I'd suspect the woman lit a cigarette and everything simply went swhoosh."

"If I might quote you from earlier," Detective Roberts said, "and your point would be?"

"It may be two counts of murder and one of lack of forethought on her part."

"Were you also responsible for the red paint splashed against the Graham home?"

"Every mystery needs a red herring," she said, chuckling at her own joke. "I came so close to saving the family reputation."

"Life's funny," Roberts said. "You caused all this misery to protect your name, and now you'll probably be going by an inmate number.

"Mrs. Childers," Anderson said gently. "How old was your son?"

"He would have been 34 this month."

"Do we also need to re-open a thirty-four-year-old case concerning a young mother's death?" Anderson asked.

"Now, this young man," Francesca said to the detective, "has a bright future with the Bureau."

Officer Anderson looked directly at Francesca Childers and spoke clearly.

"You're under arrest, Ma'am."

"I think you've made a mistake," Esther said from the doorway. "Laura's *Ma'am*. That one's *Madam.*"

"Stripes are best reserved for inmates."

35

Francesca Hortense Childers and her legal team agreed they would be unable to find a "jury of her peers" in the state of Oregon. The presiding judge sentenced her to three *consecutive* life terms in prison with a possible fourth charge pending.

Francesca is currently writing a self-help book (in perfect Palmer Penmanship) with the working title *Cell Décor for Dummies*.

- Pfeifer, Roberts, and Anderson remain in the city doing what they do best—keeping Portland safe.
- Edward, aka Wart, Simmons is now selling used cars in Milwaukie.

- Charmaigne headed for Vegas with the plumbing contractor.
- Nurse Esther wrote a "scrip" for pain killers for Vivian's recurring neck pain, and Ernie went country, whistling *God Is Great, Beer Is Good, and People Are Crazy.*
- Laura and Russ were last seen walking arm and arm at a flea market.

"A pop of color is highly over-rated for all neutral rooms—or jail cells." Laura Howard, Decorator

About this Book

Ripped, Stripped and Flipped is the second in the Designer Mystery series. It was preceded by the comic mystery novel *Hammered, Nailed and Screwed.*

The books in the series are written primarily to entertain. *Ripped, Stripped and Flipped* was also originally planned as a comic mystery romp. The finished work, however, also sheds light on a heinous crime which has remained in the shadows worldwide.

The Oregon state legislature has recognized the seriousness of human trafficking along the Interstate 5 corridor from Mexico through the state of Washington and beyond.

During the 2013 session, members of the Oregon state legislature passed a measure making conviction of the crime of sex trafficking a felony. Those convicted of benefitting financially from trafficking and knowing that another person will be subjected to involuntary servitude or coerced into commercial sex acts by force or fraud (and disregarding the fact that person is a minor) can be found guilty of a Class A felony.

The legislation was signed into law by Oregon Governor John Kitzhaber on August 1, 2013.

Acknowledgments

Thanks to family and friends who either knowingly or accidentally help to build the stories in the Designer Mystery series. One of you suggested the Street of Dreams setting for *Ripped, Stripped and Flipped*. Another mentioned the Oregon legislation addressing sex trafficking. Two of you read the manuscript in rough form and made suggestions or provided additional decorating tips. One of you listened to me test possible titles for over a year, and Kitty Buchner edited and formatted the manuscript to create the actual book. Finally, a special thank you to the readers of *Hammered, Nailed and Screwed* and members of book clubs who requested a sequel. You all know who you are, and I thank you.

The Author

Kathleen Hering resides in the towns of Albany and Jacksonville, Oregon, where she is currently plotting the next Designer Mystery. She started writing fiction after retiring from public schools where she worked as a middle school principal and district personnel director. She is married to print journalist and TV and radio news commentator Hasso Hering. They spend their leisure time riding a tandem bicycle, rowing a canoe, and enjoying their grandchildren. Not necessarily in that order. Readers can contact Kathleen Hering at:

DesignerMysteries@gmail.com .